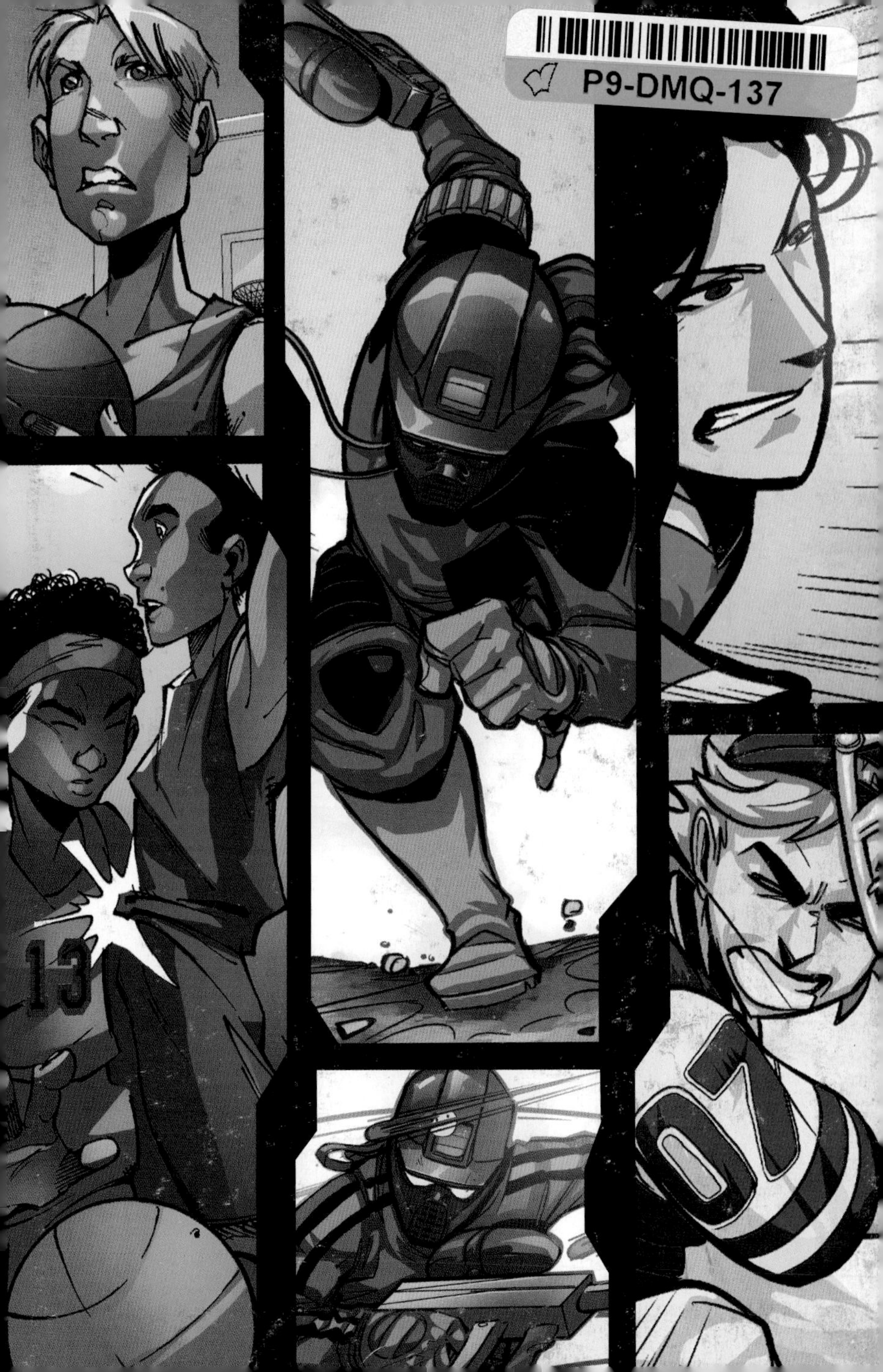
13

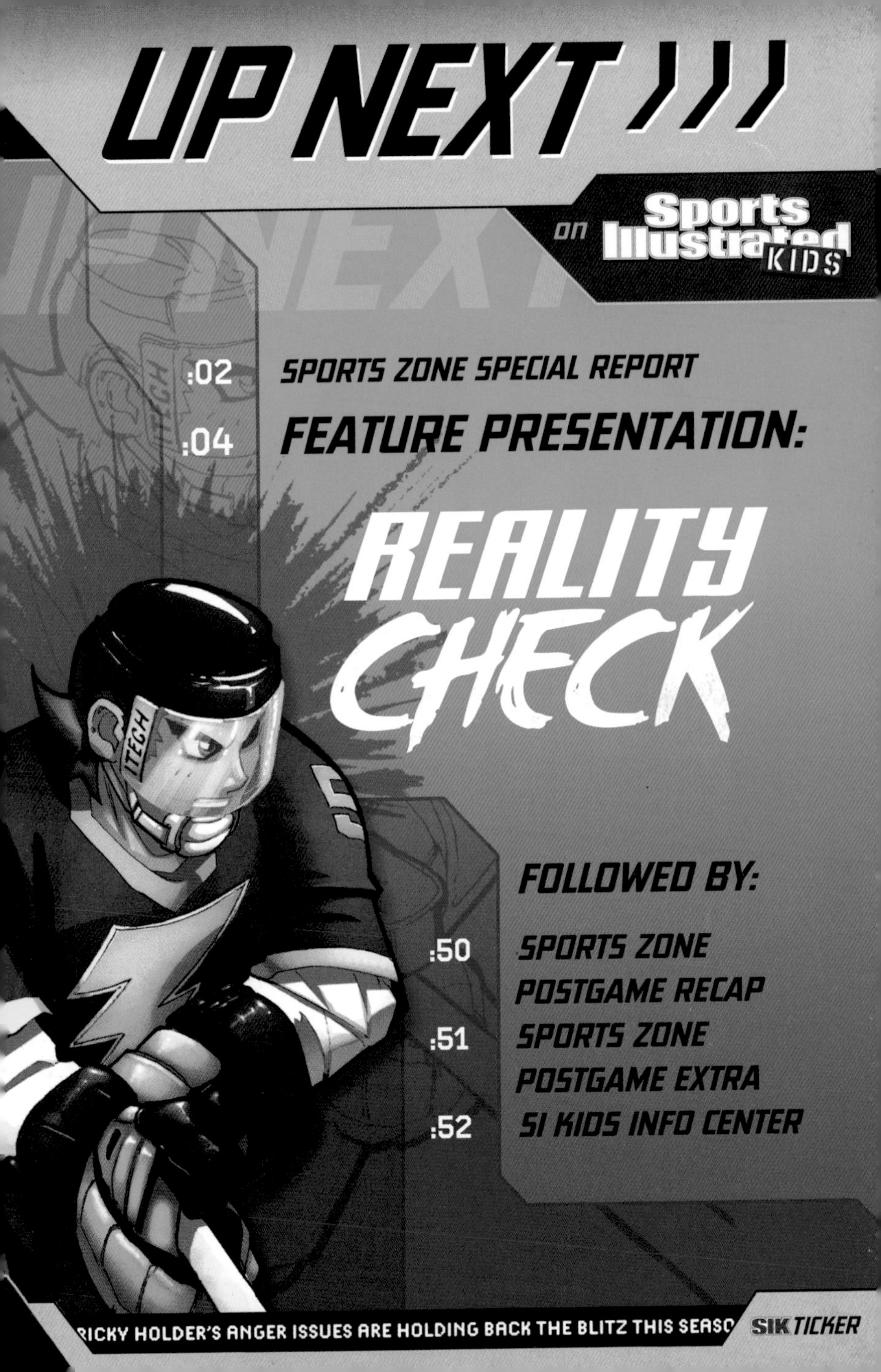
UP NEXT
on Sports Illustrated KIDS
:02 SPORTS ZONE SPECIAL REPORT
:04 FEATURE PRESENTATION:
REALITY CHECK
FOLLOWED BY:
:50 SPORTS ZONE POSTGAME RECAP
:51 SPORTS ZONE POSTGAME EXTRA
:52 SI KIDS INFO CENTER
ITECH
RICKY HOLDER'S ANGER ISSUES ARE HOLDING BACK THE BLITZ THIS SEASO
SIK TICKER

PORTS ZONE

ECIAL REPORT

BLITZ TEAM TO HOLDER: "DON'T SKATE ANGRY, RICKY!"

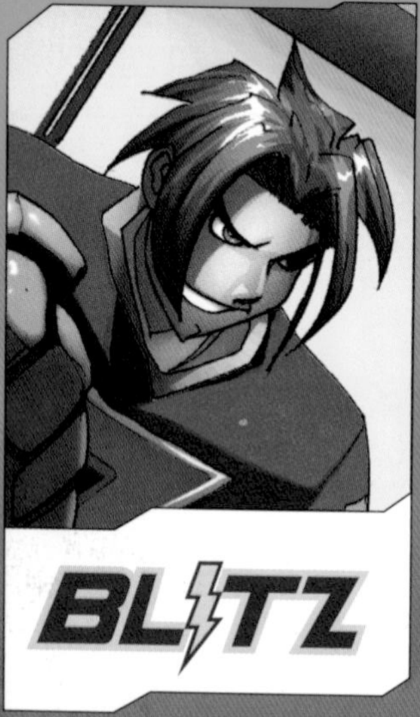
BLITZ

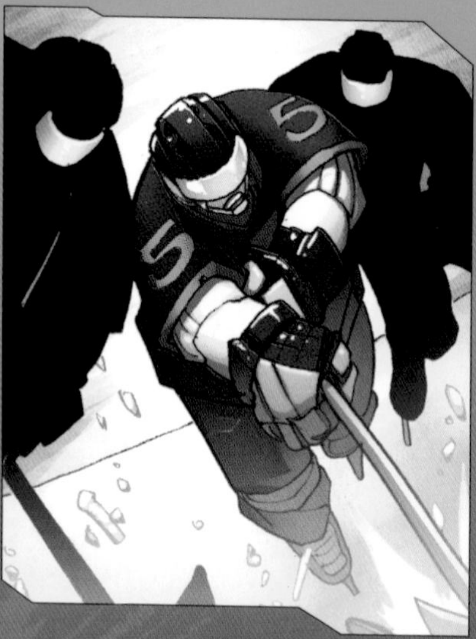

RICKY HOLDER

STATS:
AGE: 14
TEAM: BLITZ
NUMBER: 05
POSITION: DEFENSEMAN

BIO: Ricky Holder is the Blitz's best defensive player, but lately he's been all offense — and not the goal-scoring kind. Ricky's been spending more time in the penalty box than in the game, and his anger issues have put him on thin ice with his teammates. To make matters worse, Ricky's father continues to pressure Ricky to play rough, leaving the teen between the puck and a hard place.

Sports

BLZ vs BKS 3-1
TGR vs RDR 33-32
EAG vs BAN 14-7
SPA vs WLD 4-3
BAN vs RDR 21-15
RZR vs LIG 4-3

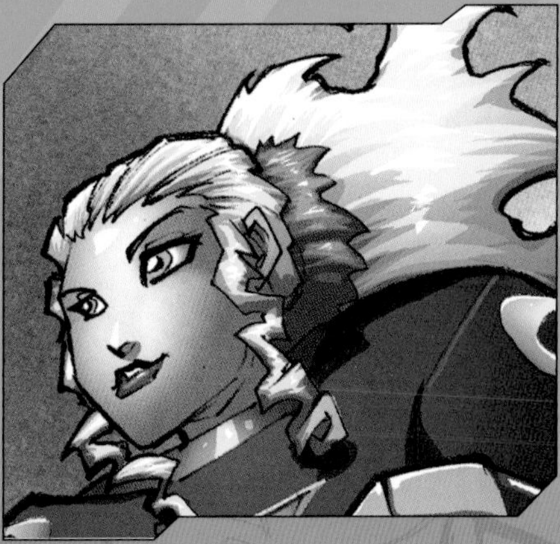

JENNIFER TAYLOR

TEAM: BLITZ
AGE: 14 **NUMBER:** 09
TEAM ROLE: CAPTAIN
POSITION: CENTER
BIO: Jen is far and away the best center in the entire state. She leads the league in assists and total points earned. It's no surprise she is the Blitz's team captain.

JACK HOLDER

TEAM: BLITZ **AGE:** 44
BIO: Mr. Holder is Ricky's father. He pushes his son to play hard and be aggressive at all times — even during practice scrimmages.

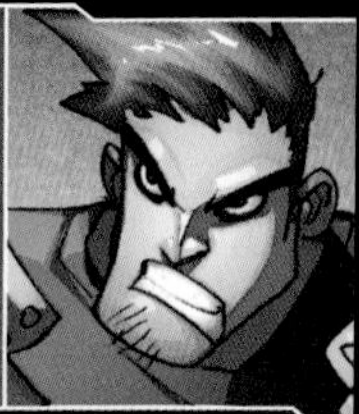

MR. HOLDER

MARK JACOBS

TEAM: BLITZ **AGE:** 13 **NO:** 17 **POSITION:** LEFT WING
BIO: Mark Jacobs is a top-notch forward. He's skilled, works hard, shares the puck, and is well-liked among his teammates.

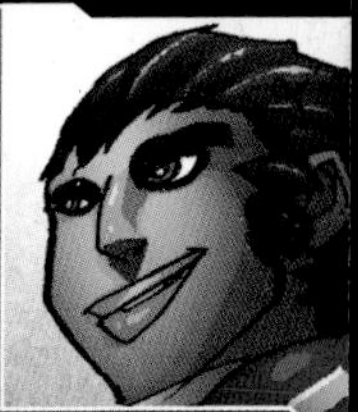

JACOBS

MICHAEL MORELLI

TEAM: BLITZ **AGE:** 42 **POSITION:** COACH
BIO: Michael Morelli is a no-nonsense hockey coach who stands for hard work, smart play — and, above all else, team unity.

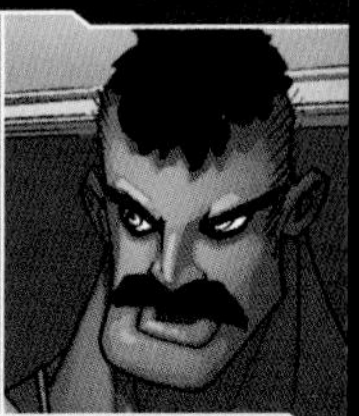

COACH

EPORTS SAY THAT THE BLITZ'S TOP SCORER IS INJURED AND OUT FOR THE SEA SIK TICKER

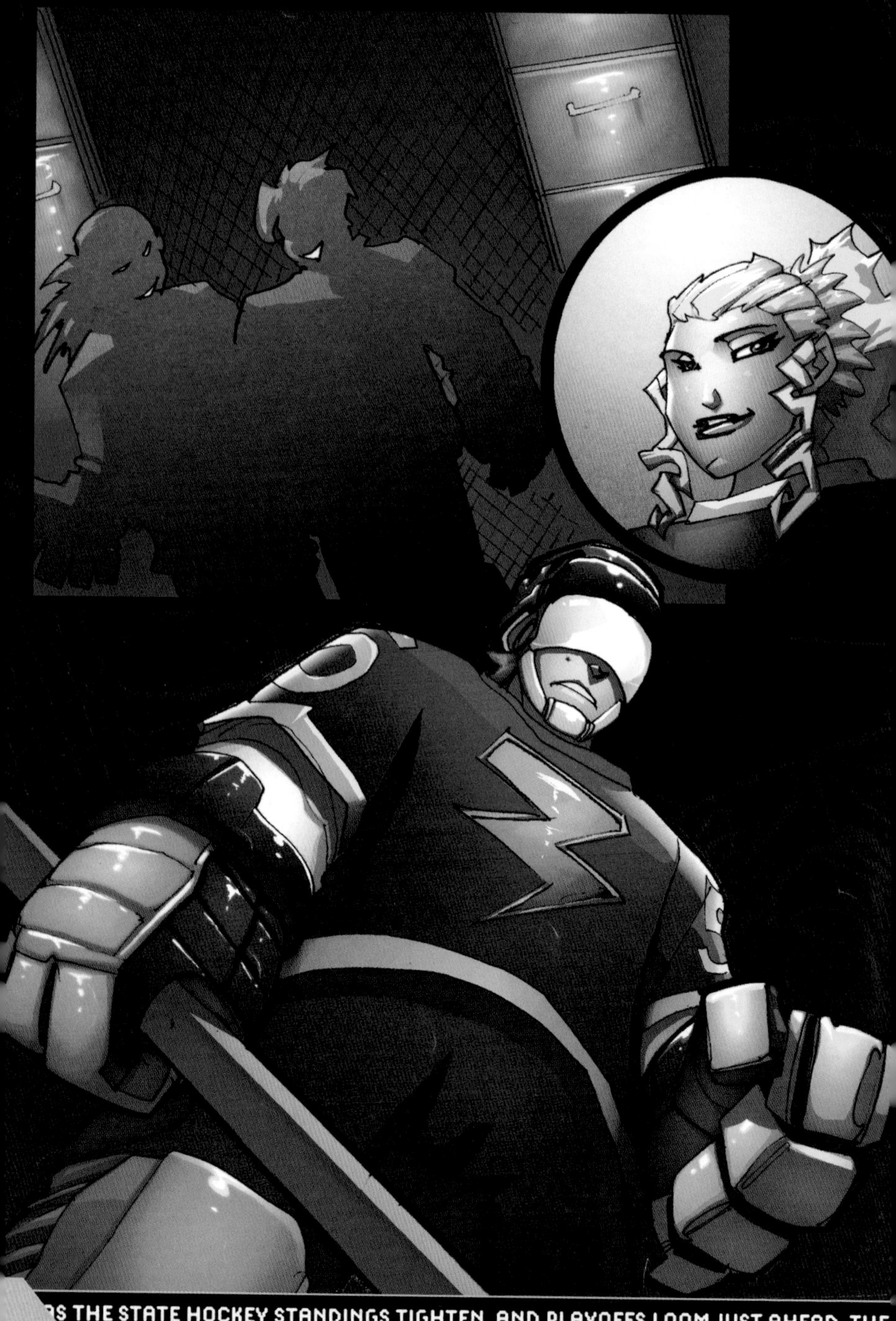

AS THE STATE HOCKEY STANDINGS TIGHTEN, AND PLAYOFFS LOOM JUST AHEAD, THE

Sports Illustrated KIDS

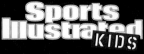

PRESENTS

REALITY CHECK

A PRODUCTION OF

STONE ARCH BOOKS
a capstone imprint

written by Nel Yomtov
illustrated by Gerardo Sandoval
colored by Benny Fuentes

designed and directed by Bob Lentz
edited by Sean Tulien
creative direction by Heather Kindseth
editorial direction by Michael Dahl

Sports Illustrated Kids *Reality Check* is published by Stone Arch Books,
151 Good Counsel Drive, P.O. Box 669,
Mankato, Minnesota 56002.
www.capstonepub.com

Summary: When he's playing hockey, Ricky Holder hits hard and never holds back. During a scrimmage, Ricky injures his own team's top scorer. Ricky's father is proud of him, but his teammates ditch him because of his dangerous checks. Ricky tries to ease up a little, but his teammates won't forgive him, and his father is mad that he's not playing aggressively. Can Ricky fix things before the state's toughest team comes to town?

Cataloging-in-Publication data is available on the Library of Congress website.

ISBN: 978-1-4342-1912-1 (library binding)
ISBN: 978-1-4342-2294-7 (paperback)

Printed in the United States of America in Stevens Point, Wisconsin.
092009 005619WZS10

HOPE TO BREAK FREE FROM THE PACK AND BECOME THE NUMBER ONE SEE SIK TICKER

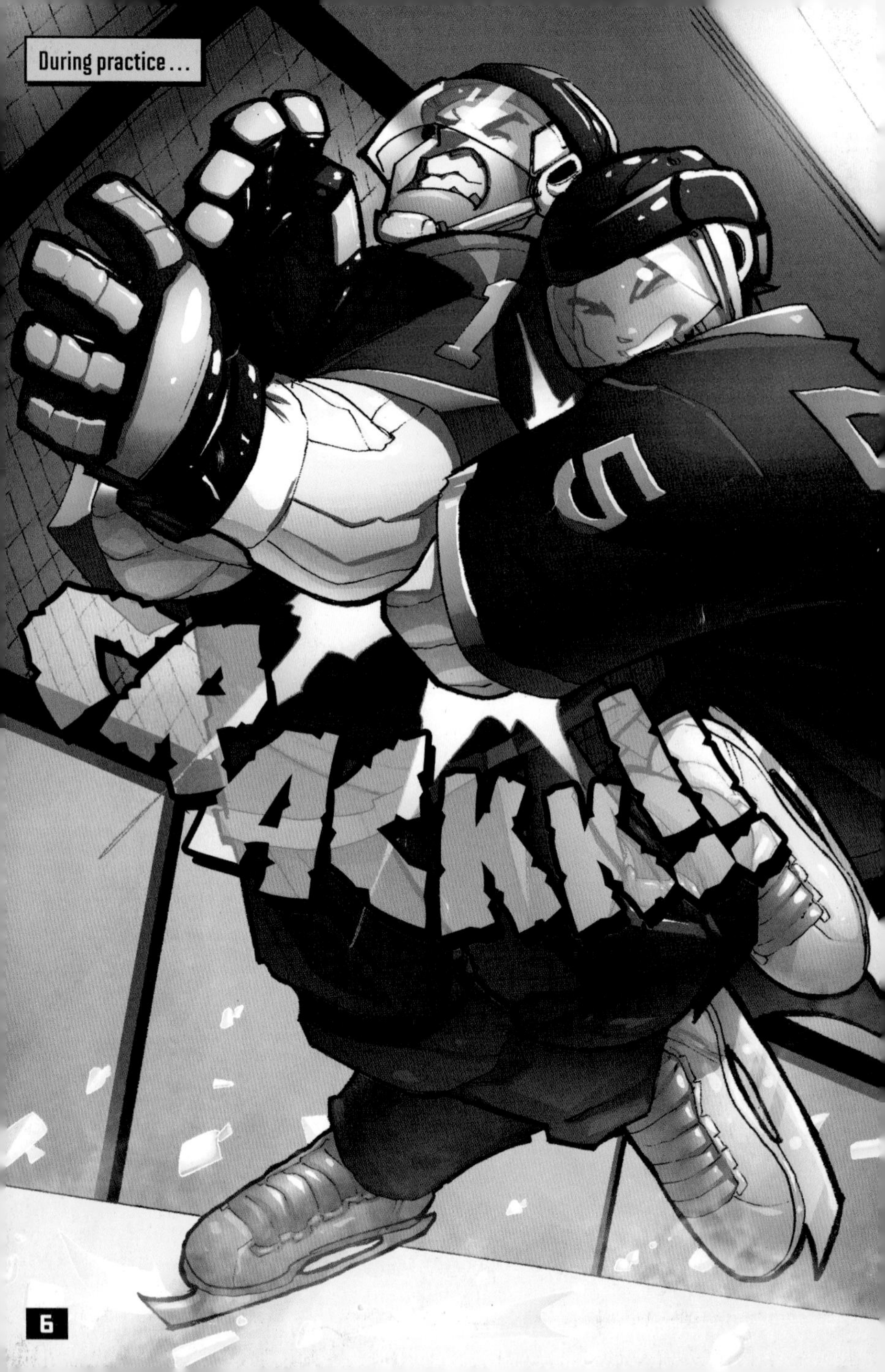
During practice . . .

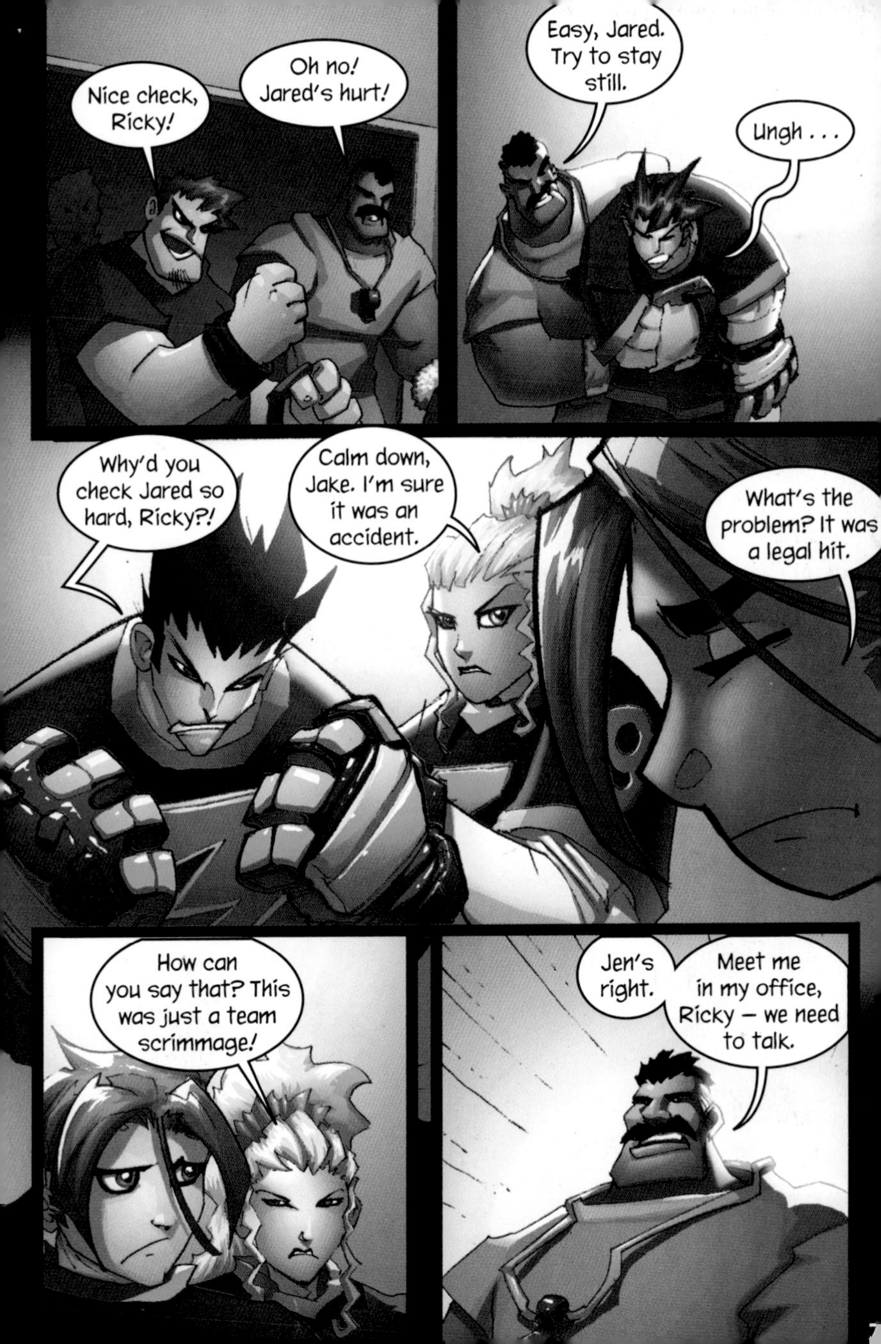

Nice check, Ricky!
Oh no! Jared's hurt!
Easy, Jared. Try to stay still.
Ungh . . .
Why'd you check Jared so hard, Ricky?!
Calm down, Jake. I'm sure it was an accident.
What's the problem? It was a legal hit.
How can you say that? This was just a team scrimmage!
Jen's right.
Meet me in my office, Ricky — we need to talk.

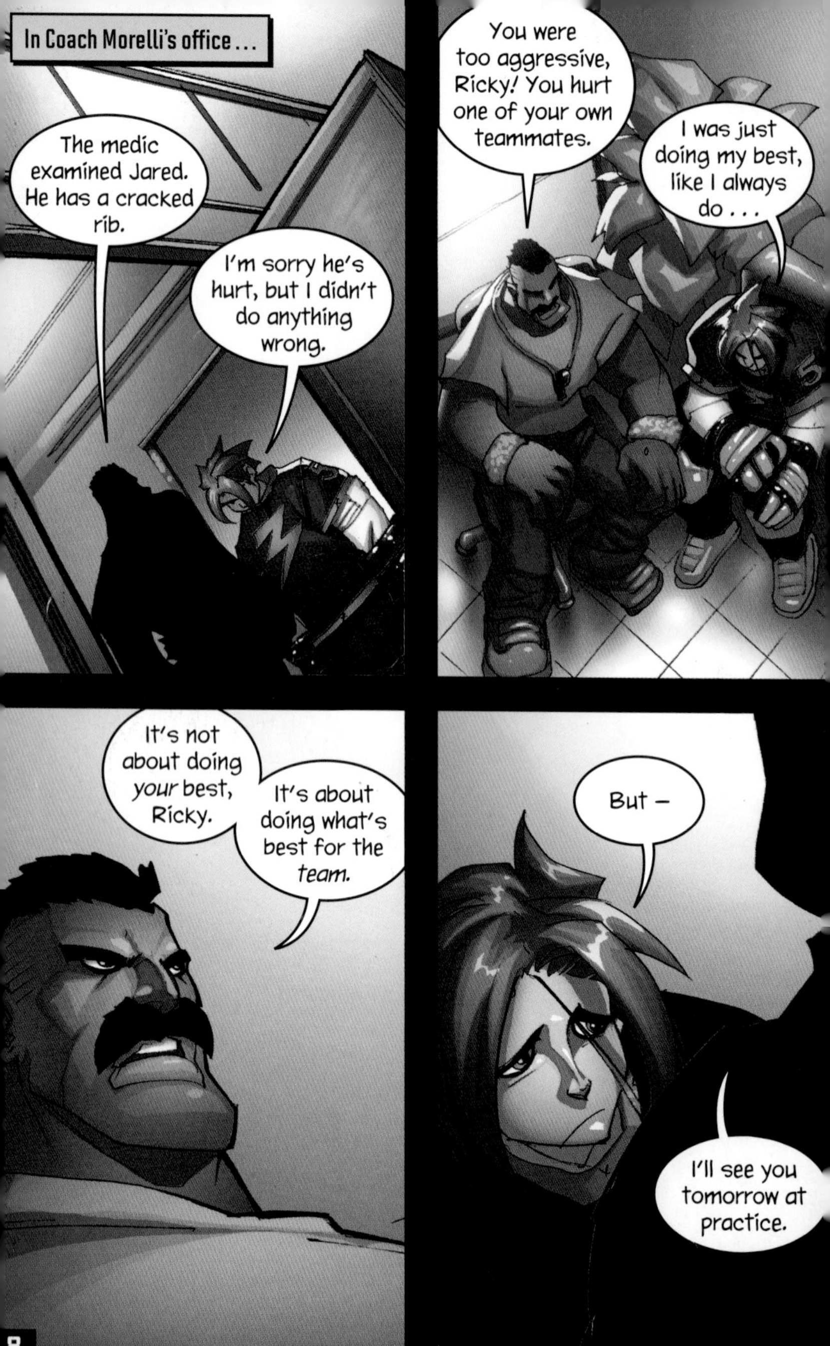
In Coach Morelli's office . . .
The medic examined Jared. He has a cracked rib.
I'm sorry he's hurt, but I didn't do anything wrong.
You were too aggressive, Ricky! You hurt one of your own teammates.
I was just doing my best, like I always do . . .
It's not about doing *your* best, Ricky.
It's about doing what's best for the *team.*
But –
I'll see you tomorrow at practice.

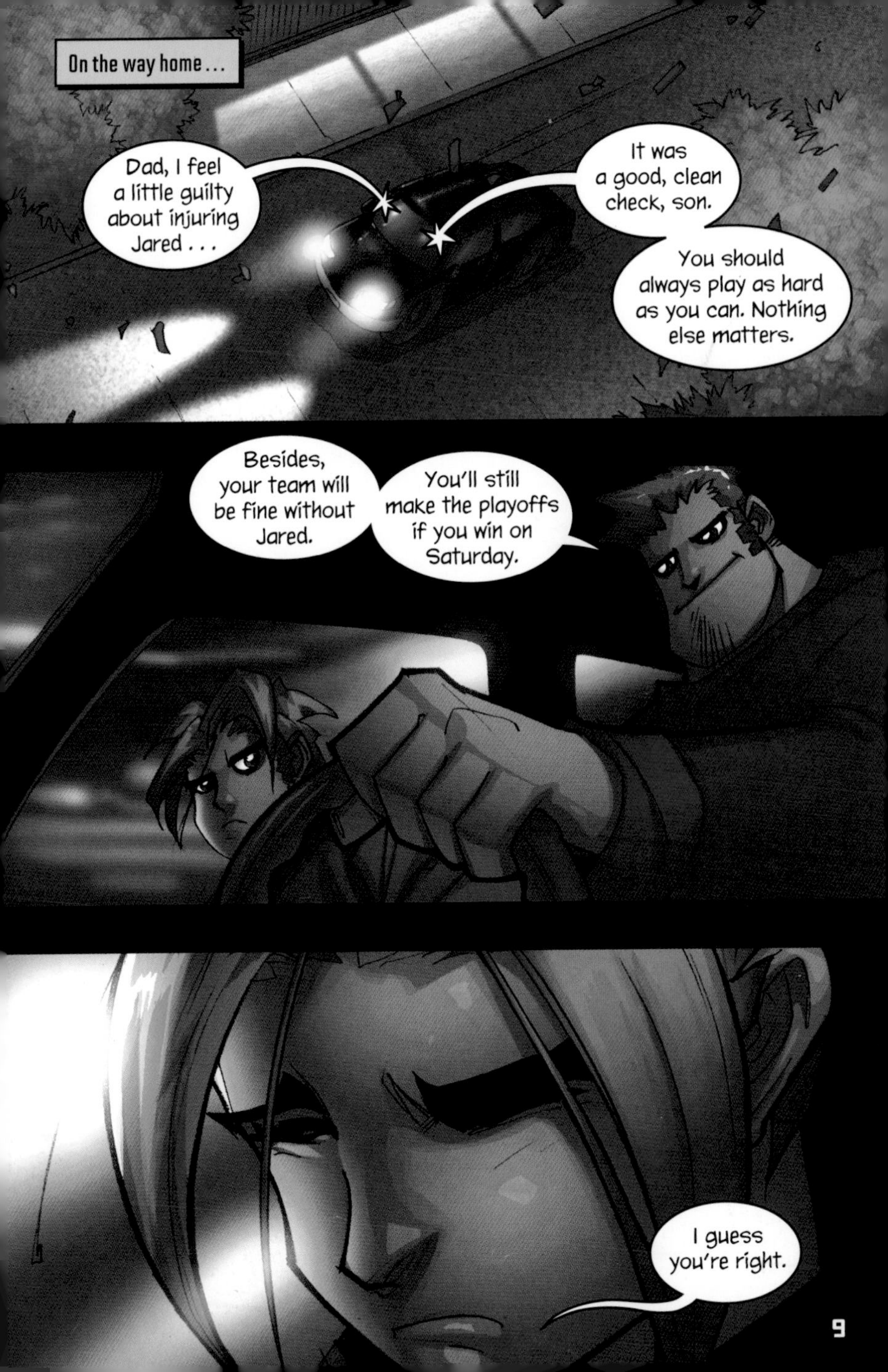
On the way home . . .
Dad, I feel a little guilty about injuring Jared . . .
It was a good, clean check, son.
You should always play as hard as you can. Nothing else matters.
Besides, your team will be fine without Jared.
You'll still make the playoffs if you win on Saturday.
I guess you're right.

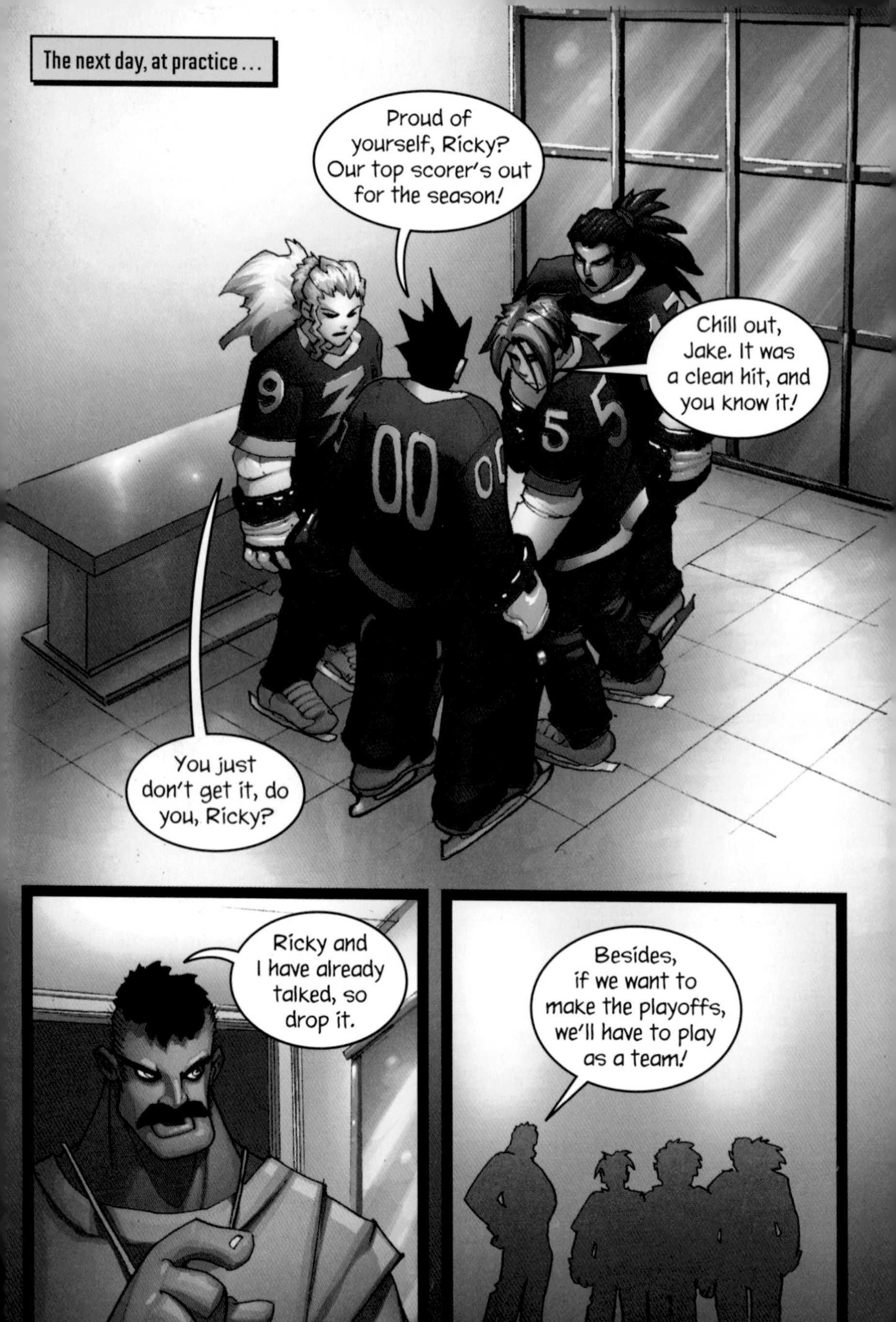
The next day, at practice . . .
Proud of yourself, Ricky? Our top scorer's out for the season!
Chill out, Jake. It was a clean hit, and you know it!
You just don't get it, do you, Ricky?
Ricky and I have already talked, so drop it.
Besides, if we want to make the playoffs, we'll have to play as a team!

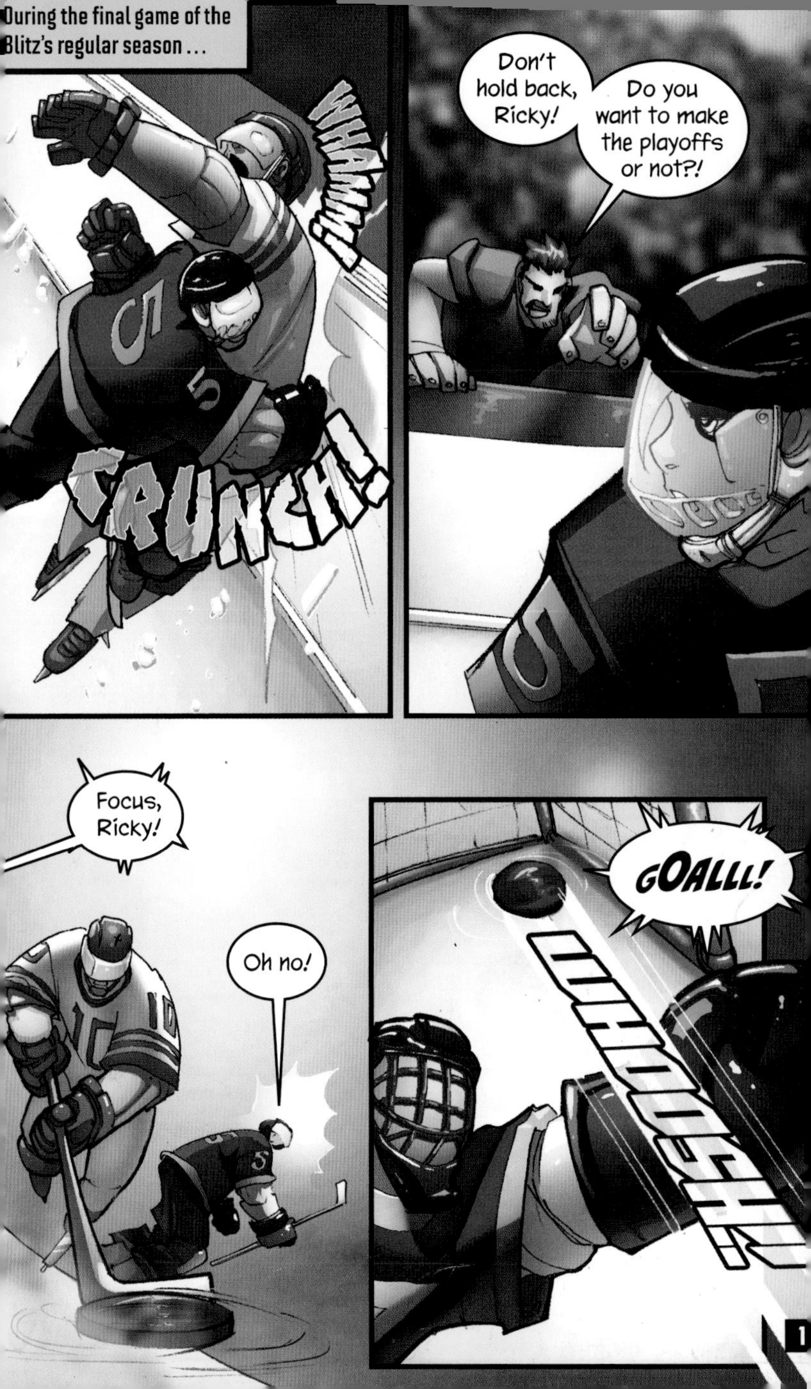
During the final game of the Blitz's regular season . . .
WHAMM!
CRUNCH!
Don't hold back, Ricky!
Do you want to make the playoffs or not?!
Focus, Ricky!
Oh no!
GOALLL!
WHOOSH!

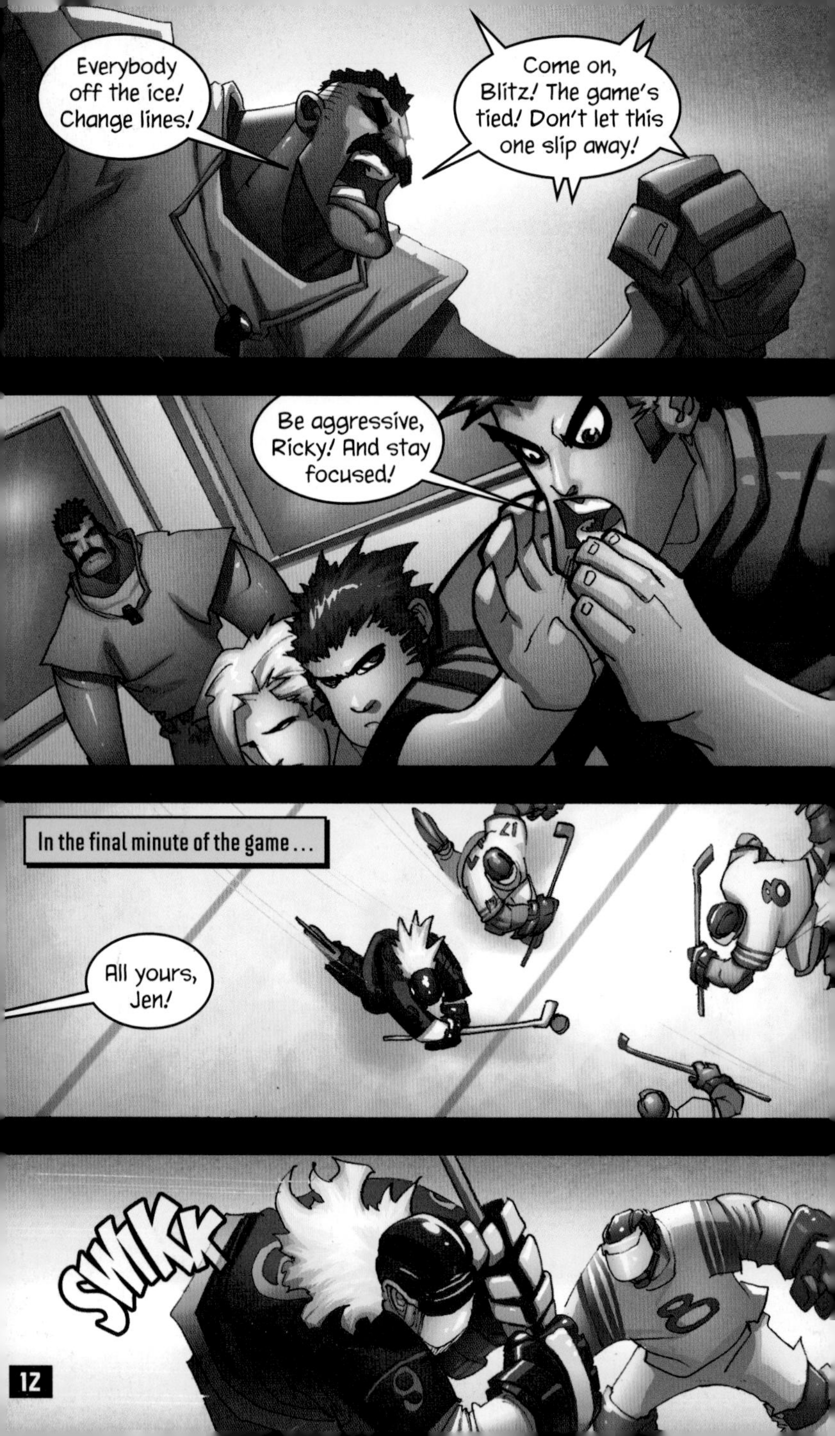

Everybody off the ice! Change lines!
Come on, Blitz! The game's tied! Don't let this one slip away!
Be aggressive, Ricky! And stay focused!
In the final minute of the game . . .
All yours, Jen!
SWIKK

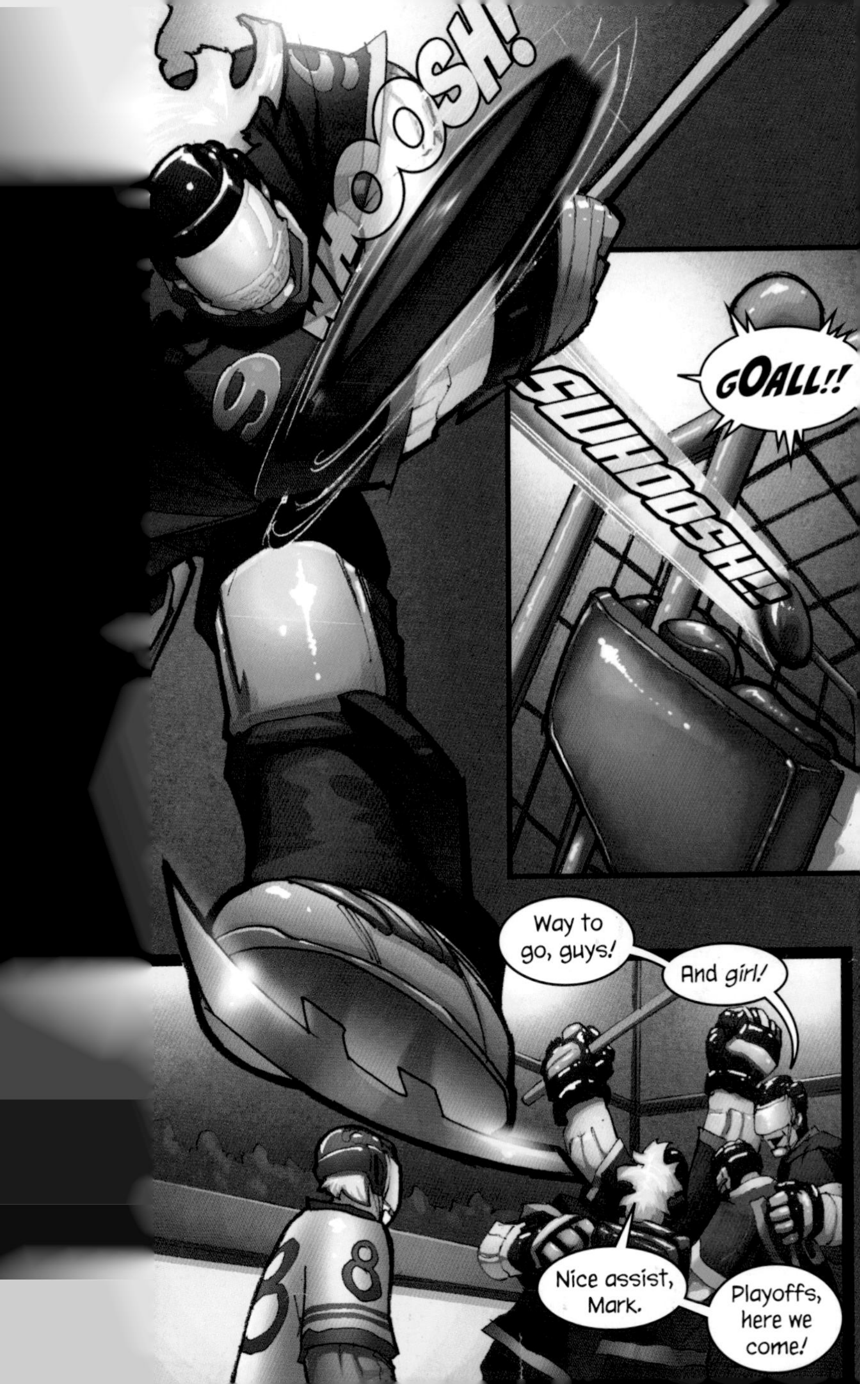
WHOOSH!
GOALL!!
SWOOSH!
Way to go, guys!
And girl!
Nice assist, Mark.
Playoffs, here we come!

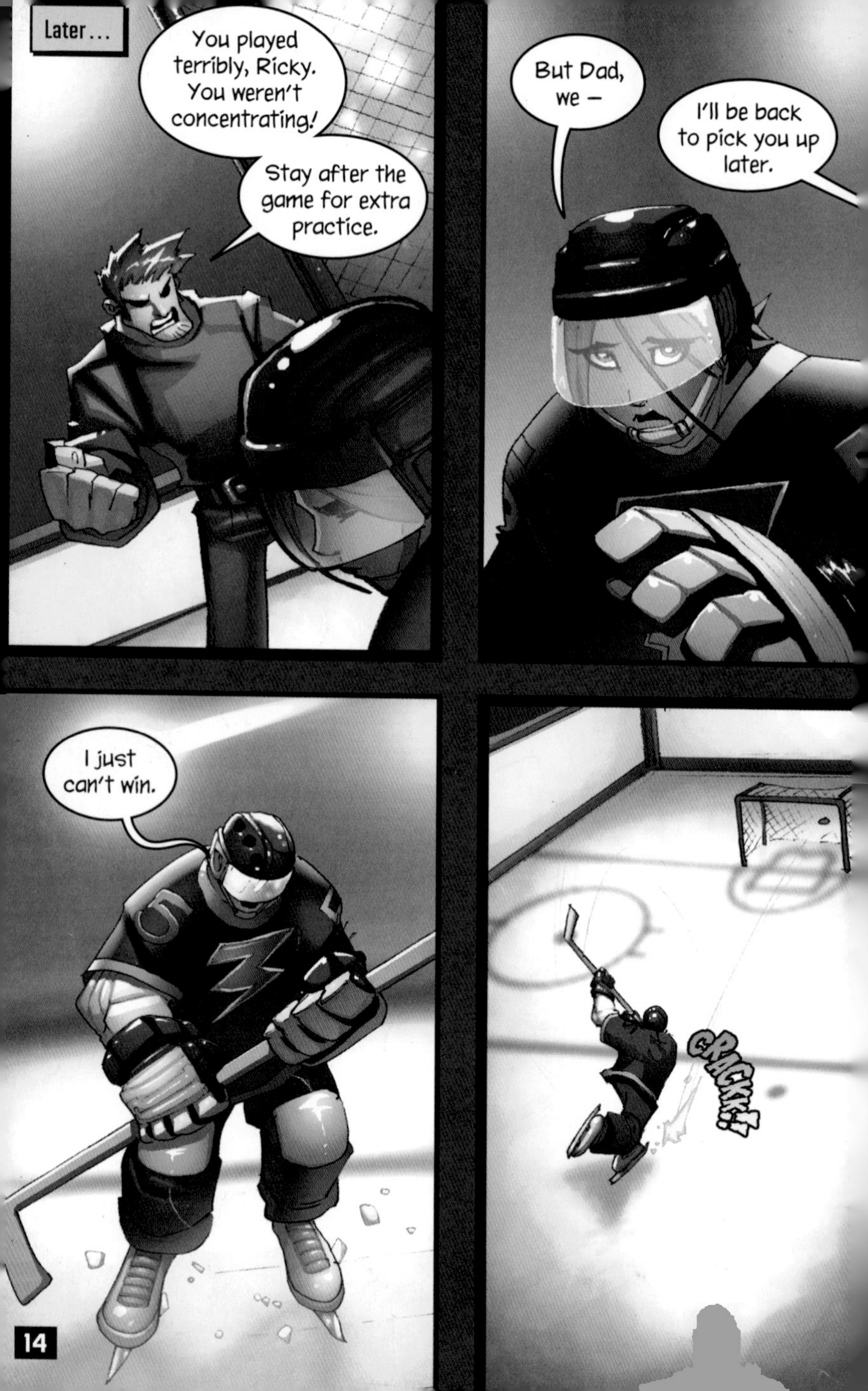
Later...
You played terribly, Ricky. You weren't concentrating!
Stay after the game for extra practice.
But Dad, we –
I'll be back to pick you up later.
I just can't win.
CRACK!!

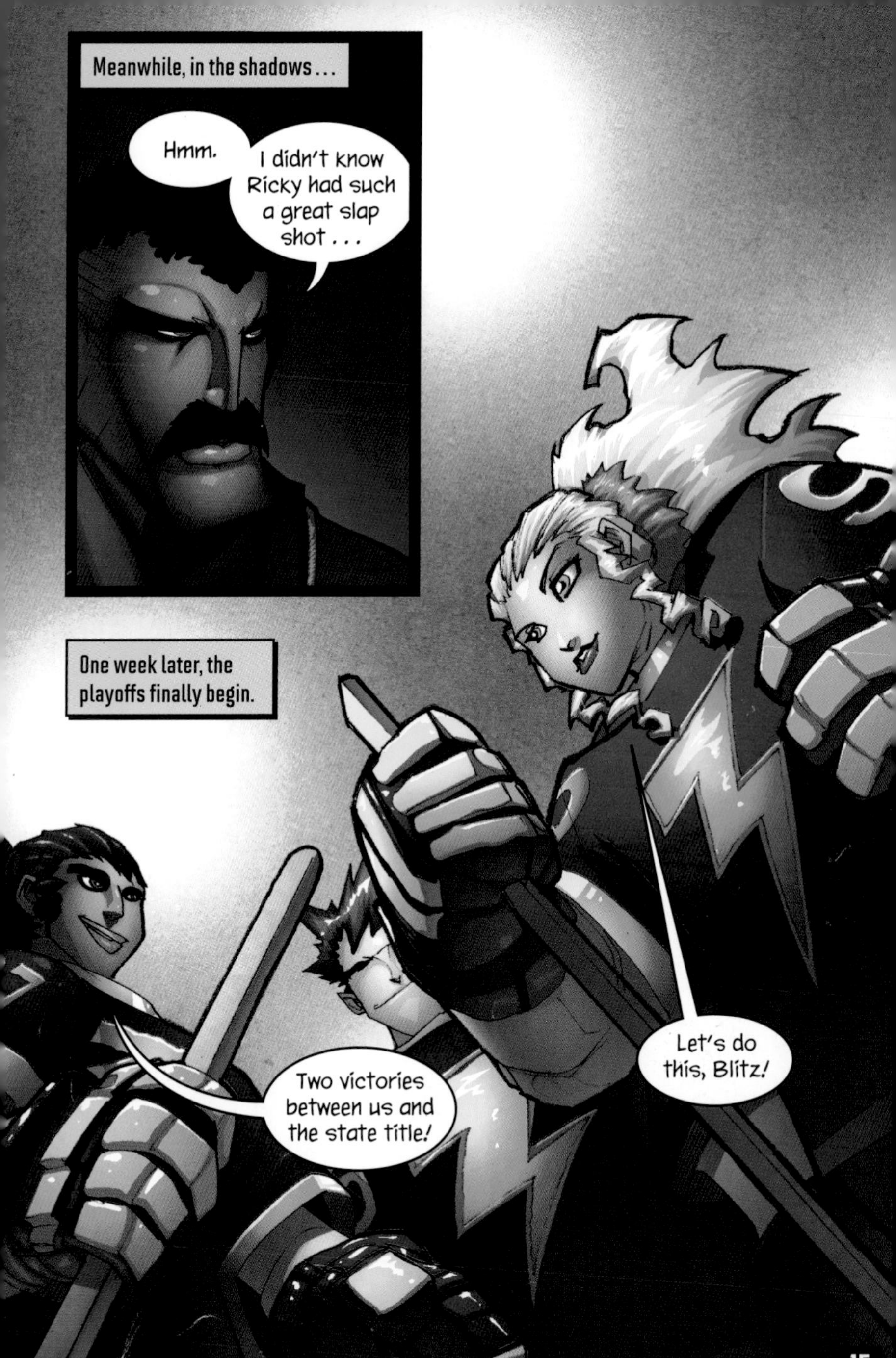
Meanwhile, in the shadows . . .
Hmm.
I didn't know Ricky had such a great slap shot . . .
One week later, the playoffs finally begin.
Two victories between us and the state title!
Let's do this, Blitz!

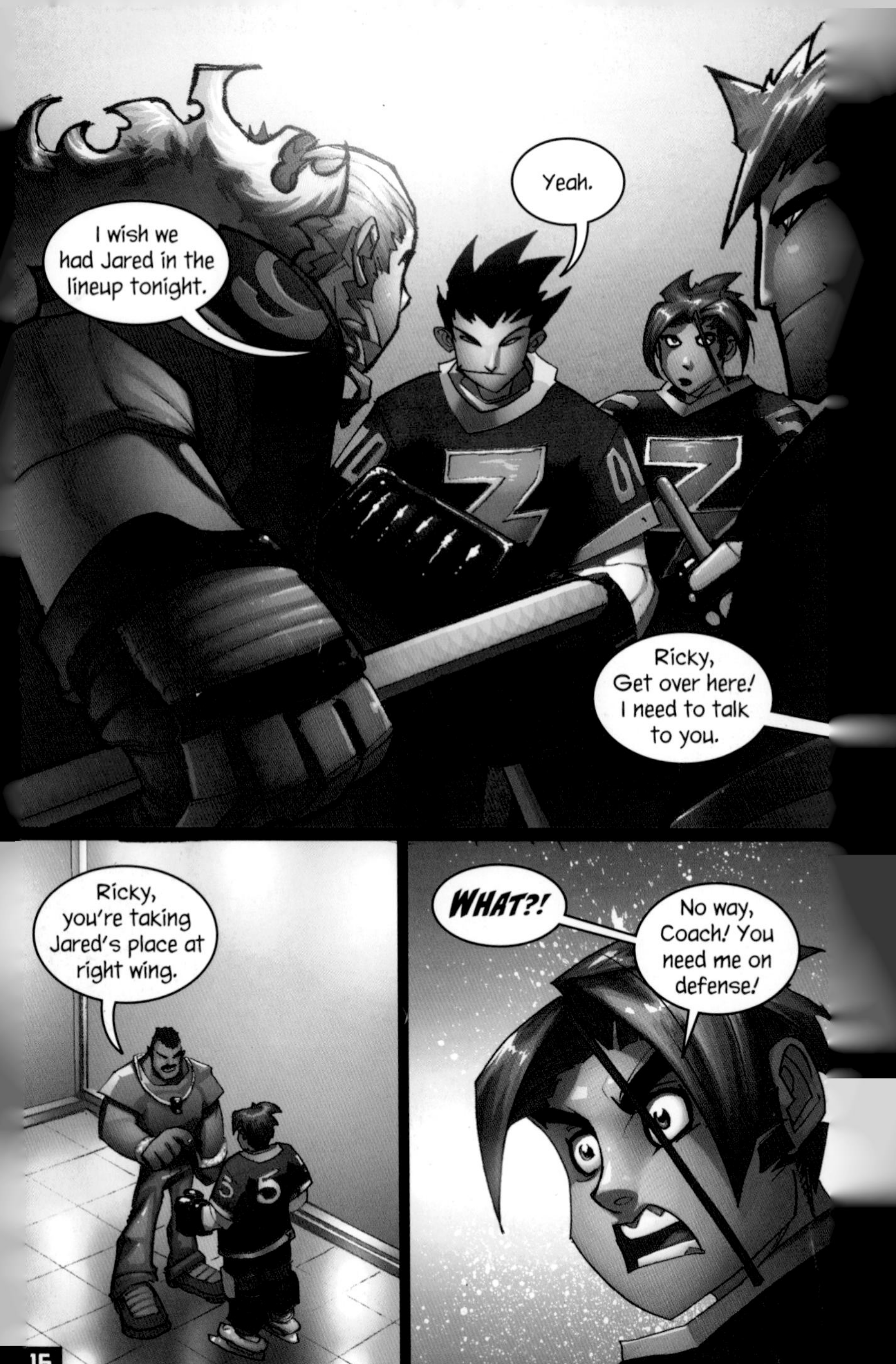
I wish we had Jared in the lineup tonight.
Yeah.
Ricky, Get over here! I need to talk to you.
Ricky, you're taking Jared's place at right wing.
WHAT?!
No way, Coach! You need me on defense!

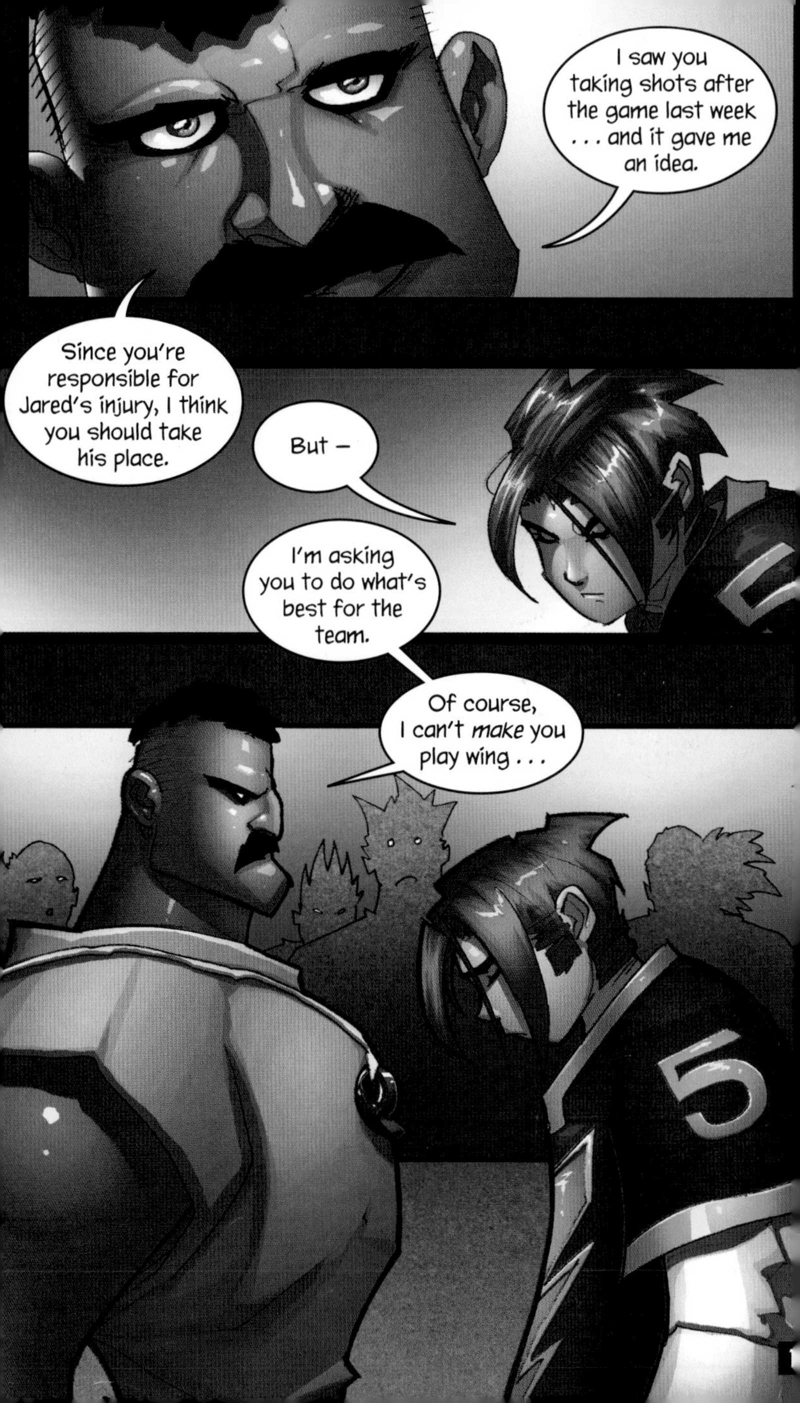
I saw you taking shots after the game last week . . . and it gave me an idea.
Since you're responsible for Jared's injury, I think you should take his place.
But –
I'm asking you to do what's best for the team.
Of course, I can't *make* you play wing . . .

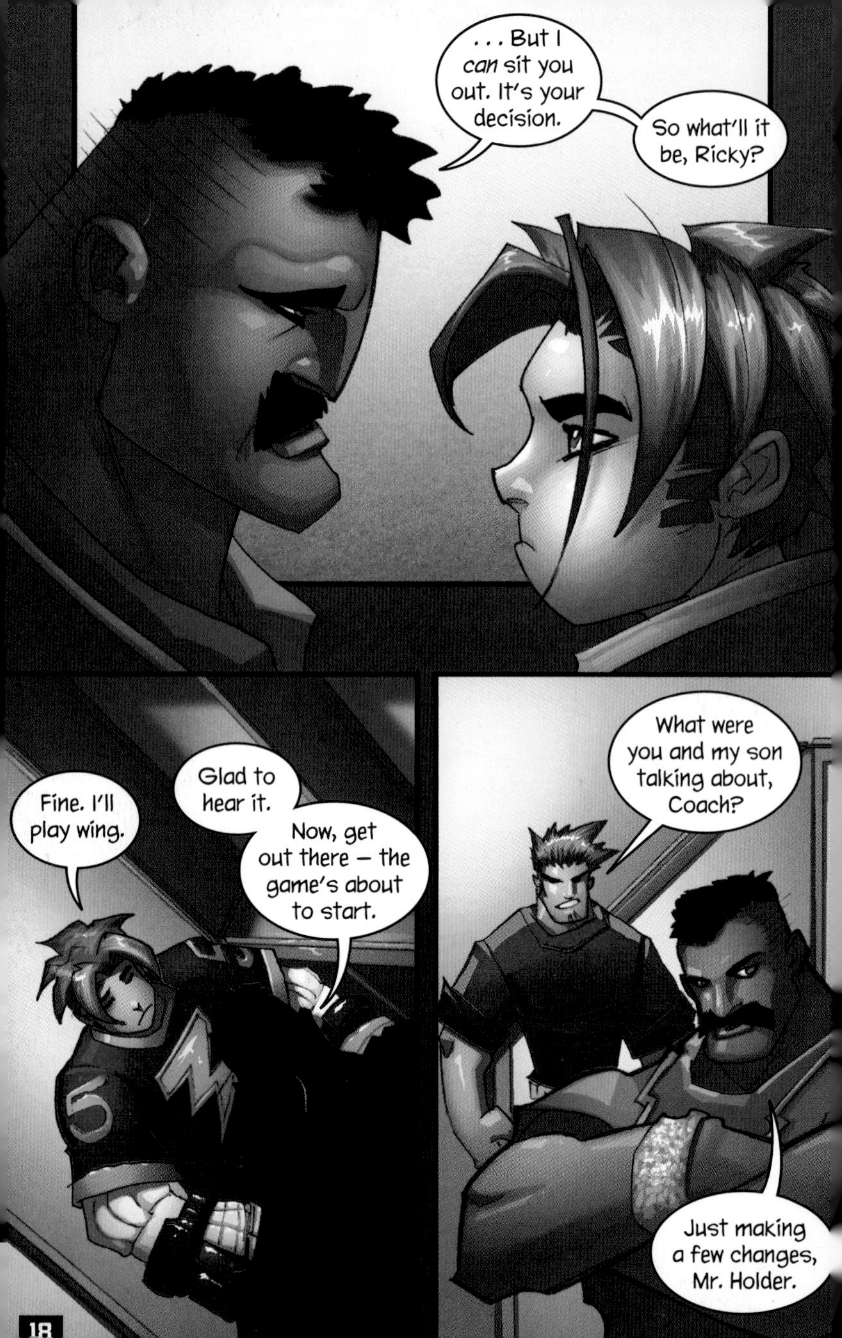
. . . But I *can* sit you out. It's your decision.
So what'll it be, Ricky?
Fine. I'll play wing.
Glad to hear it.
Now, get out there — the game's about to start.
What were you and my son talking about, Coach?
Just making a few changes, Mr. Holder.

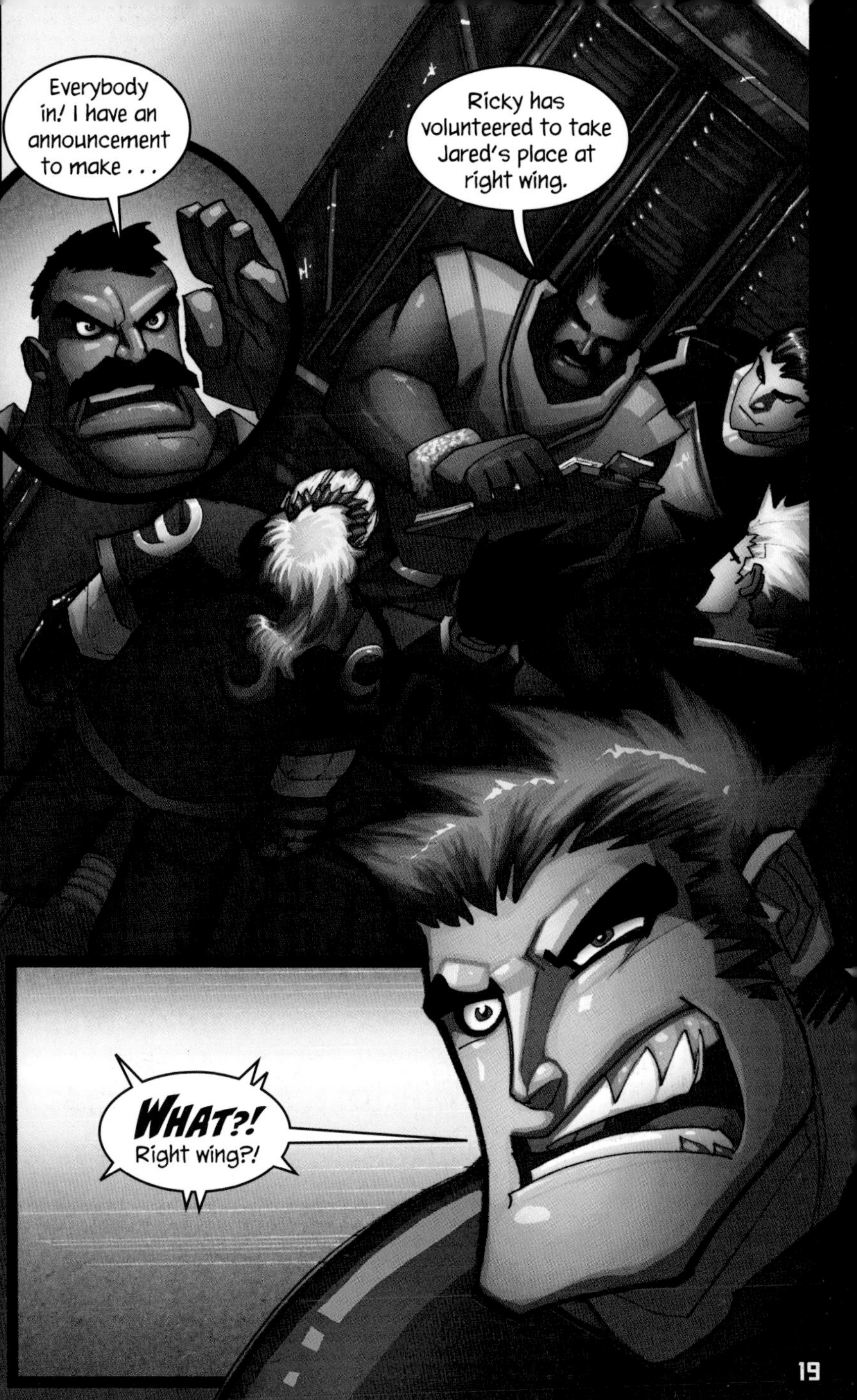
Everybody in! I have an announcement to make . . .
Ricky has volunteered to take Jared's place at right wing.
WHAT?! Right wing?!

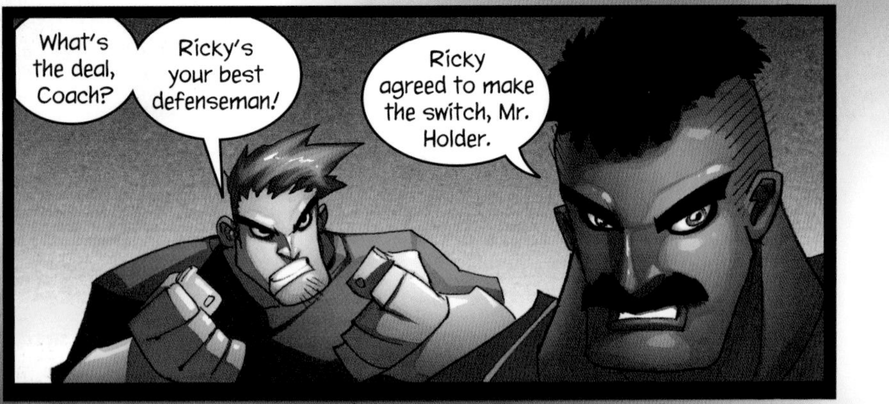
What's the deal, Coach?
Ricky's your best defenseman!
Ricky agreed to make the switch, Mr. Holder.

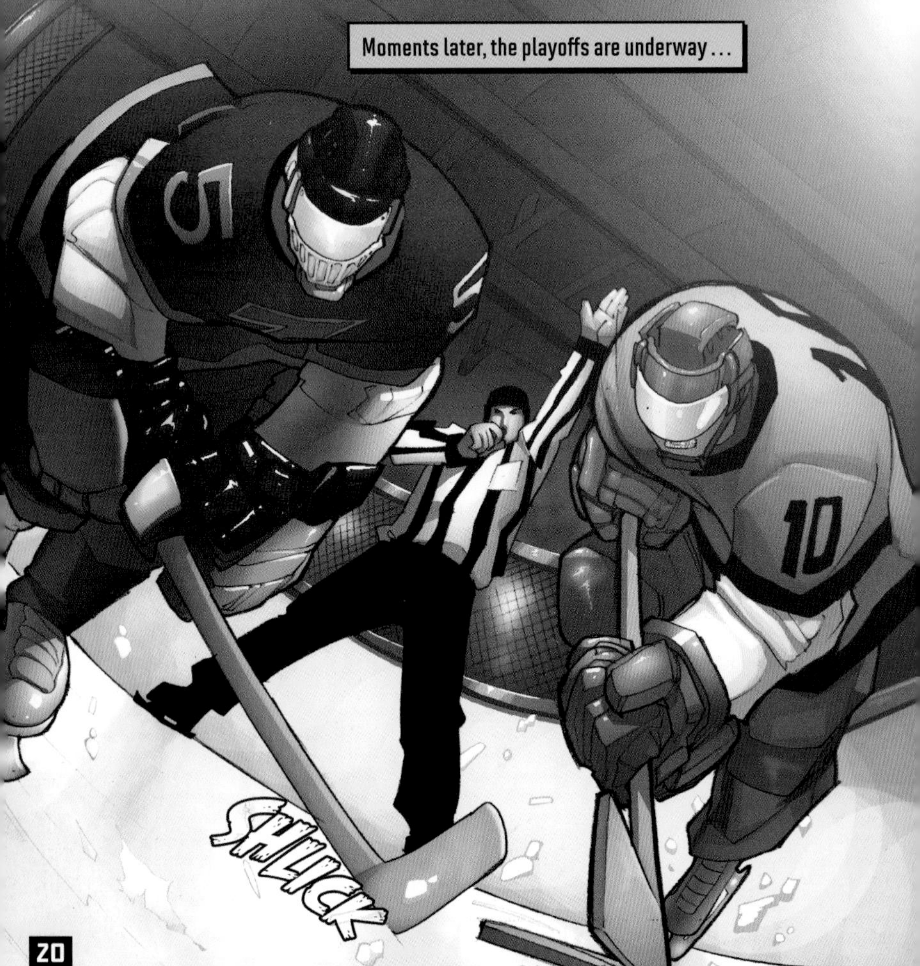
Moments later, the playoffs are underway . . .
5
10
SHLICK

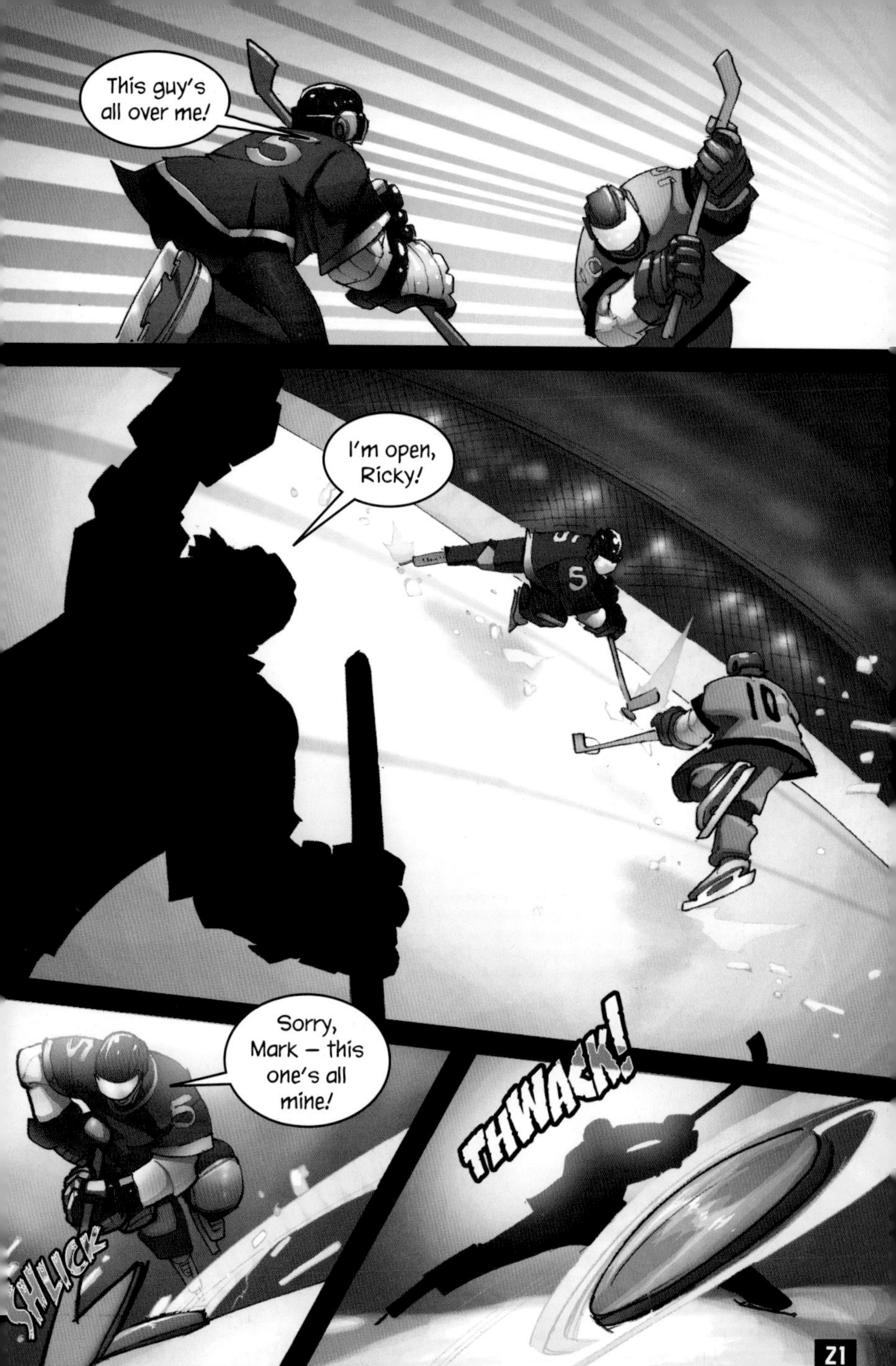
This guy's all over me!
I'm open, Ricky!
Sorry, Mark – this one's all mine!
THWACK!
SHLICK

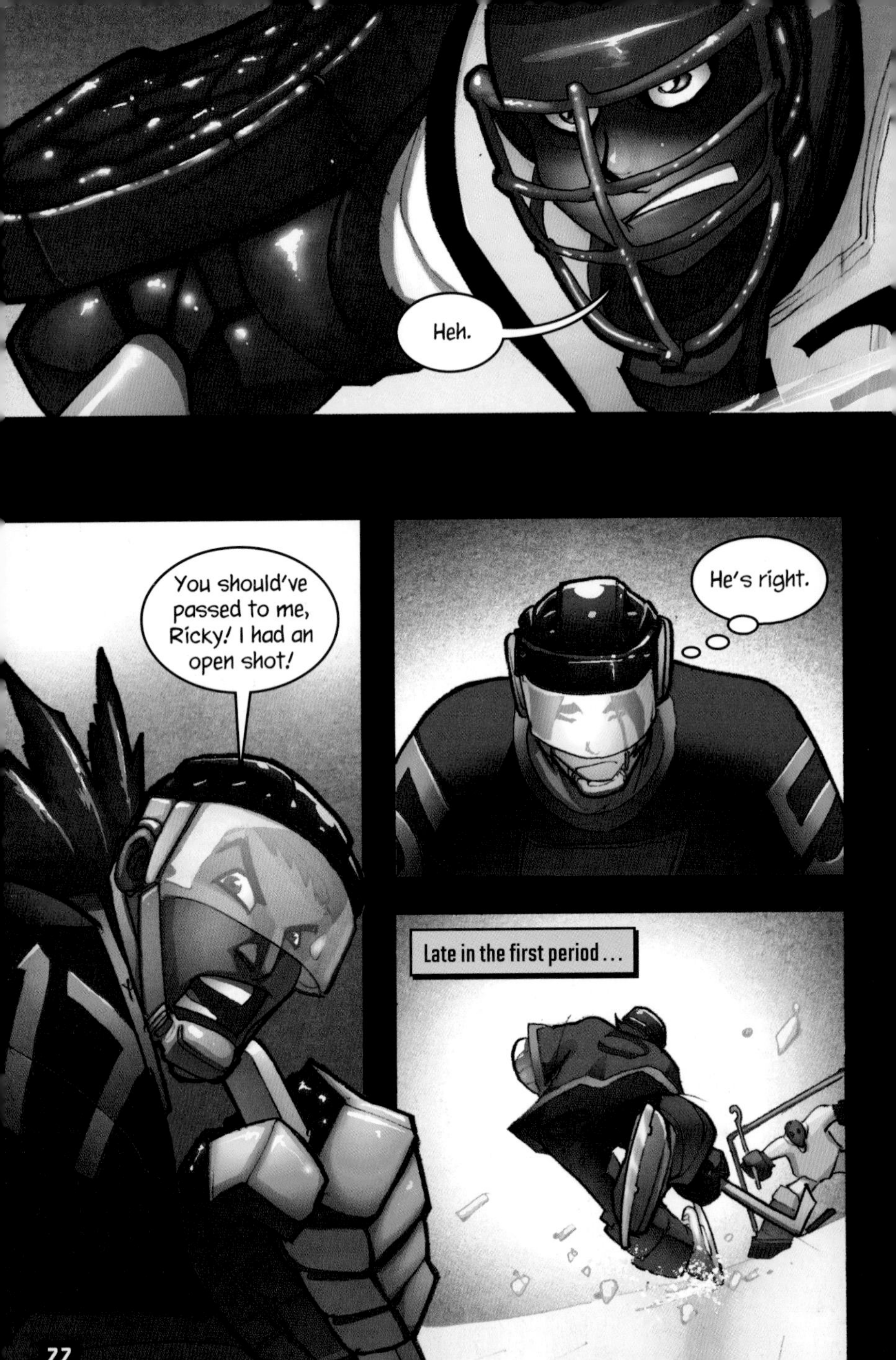
Heh.
You should've passed to me, Ricky! I had an open shot!
He's right.
Late in the first period . . .

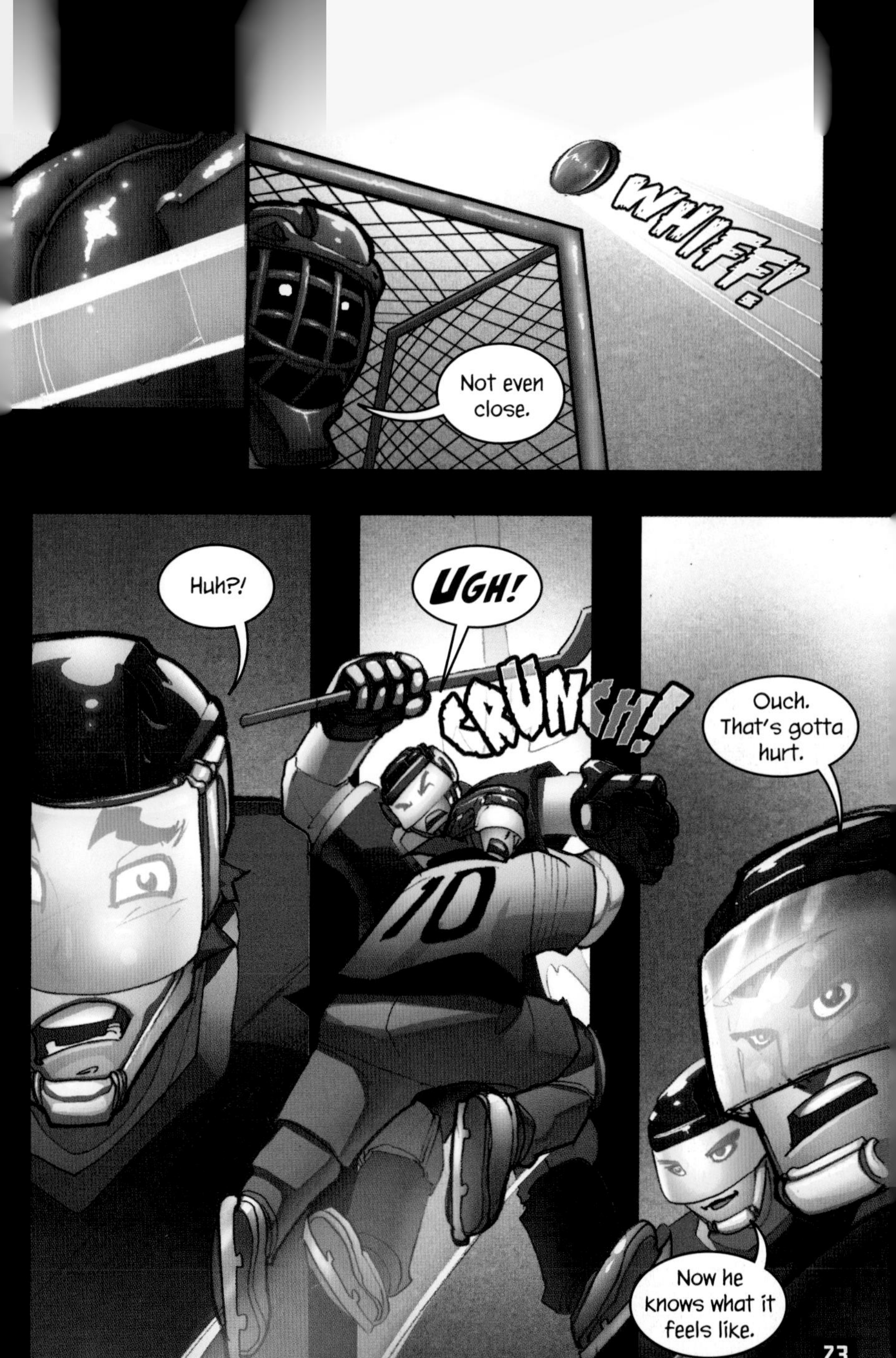
WHIFF!
Not even close.
Huh?!
UGH!
CRUNCH!
Ouch. That's gotta hurt.
Now he knows what it feels like.

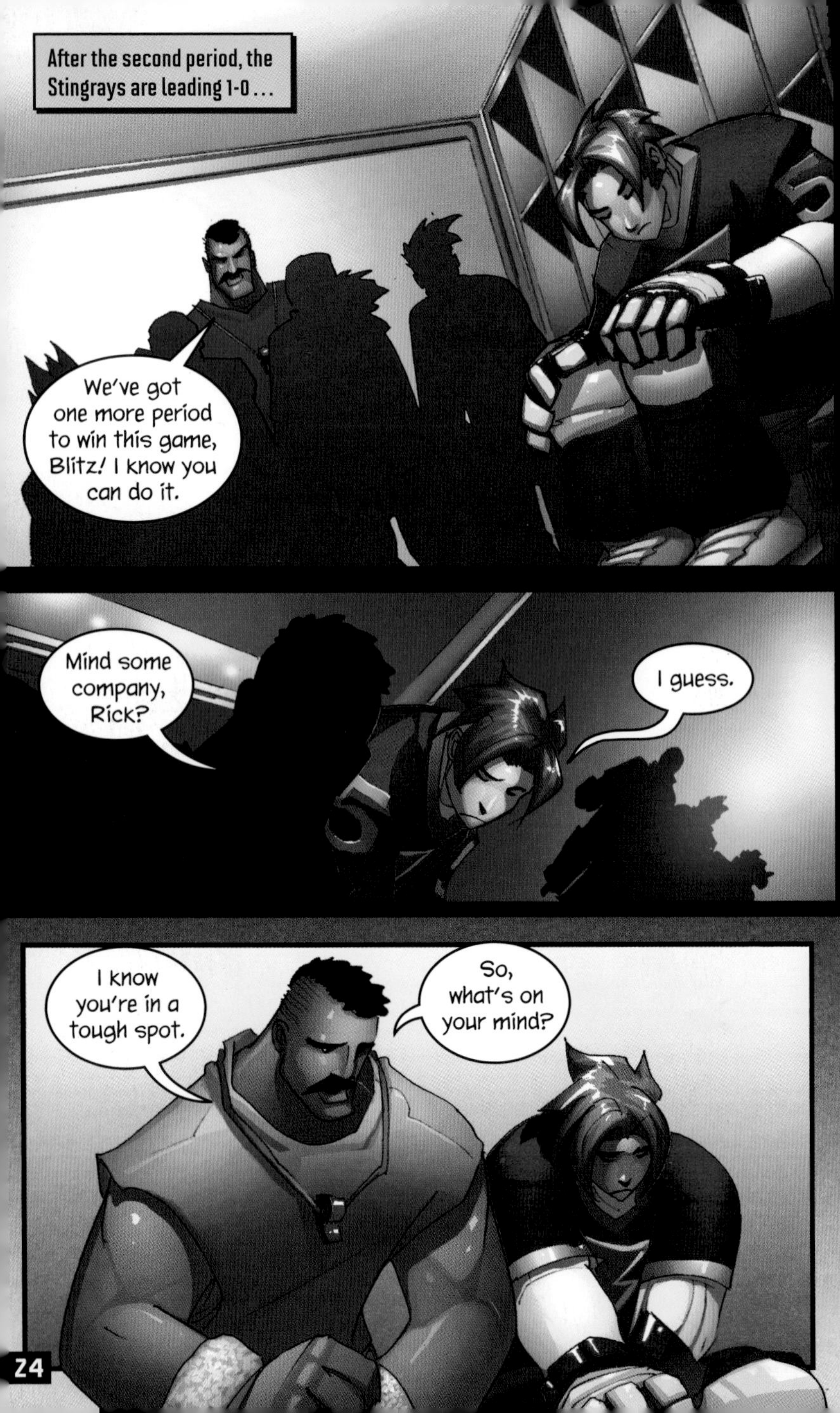
After the second period, the Stingrays are leading 1-0 . . .
We've got one more period to win this game, Blitz! I know you can do it.
Mind some company, Rick?
I guess.
I know you're in a tough spot.
So, what's on your mind?

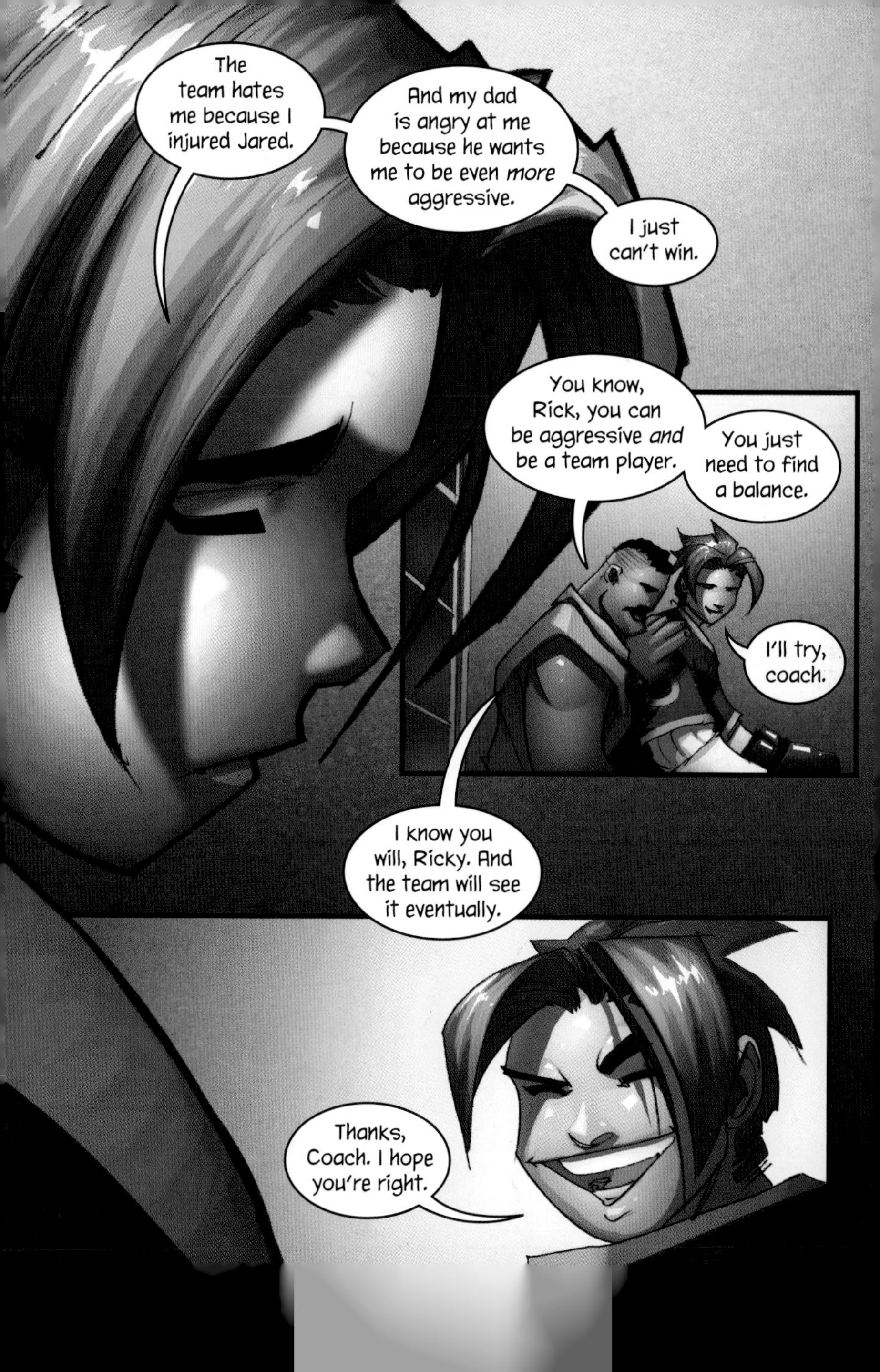
The team hates me because I injured Jared.
And my dad is angry at me because he wants me to be even *more* aggressive.
I just can't win.
You know, Rick, you can be aggressive *and* be a team player.
You just need to find a balance.
I'll try, coach.
I know you will, Ricky. And the team will see it eventually.
Thanks, Coach. I hope you're right.

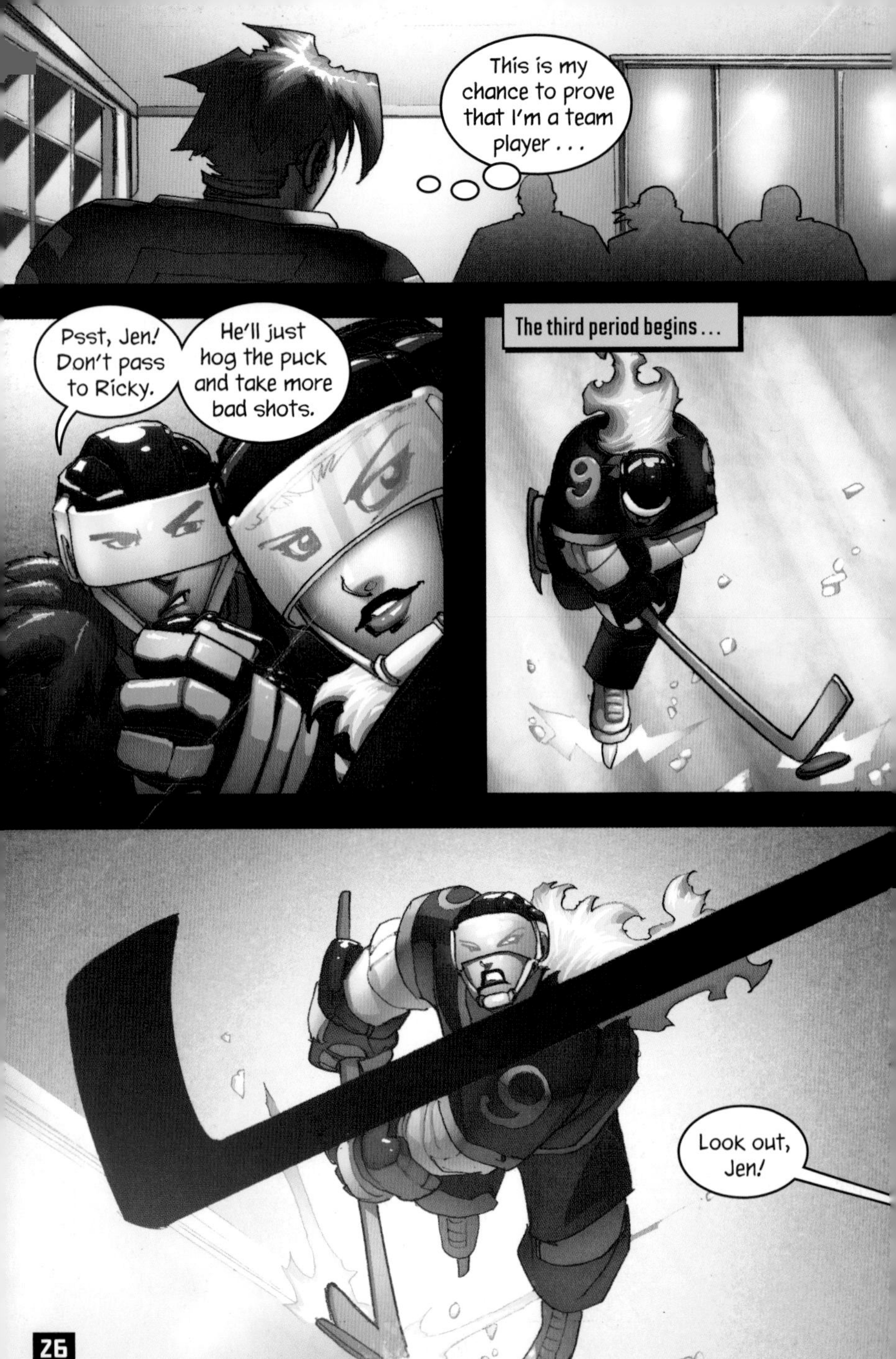
This is my chance to prove that I'm a team player . . .
Psst, Jen! Don't pass to Ricky.
He'll just hog the puck and take more bad shots.
The third period begins . . .
Look out, Jen!

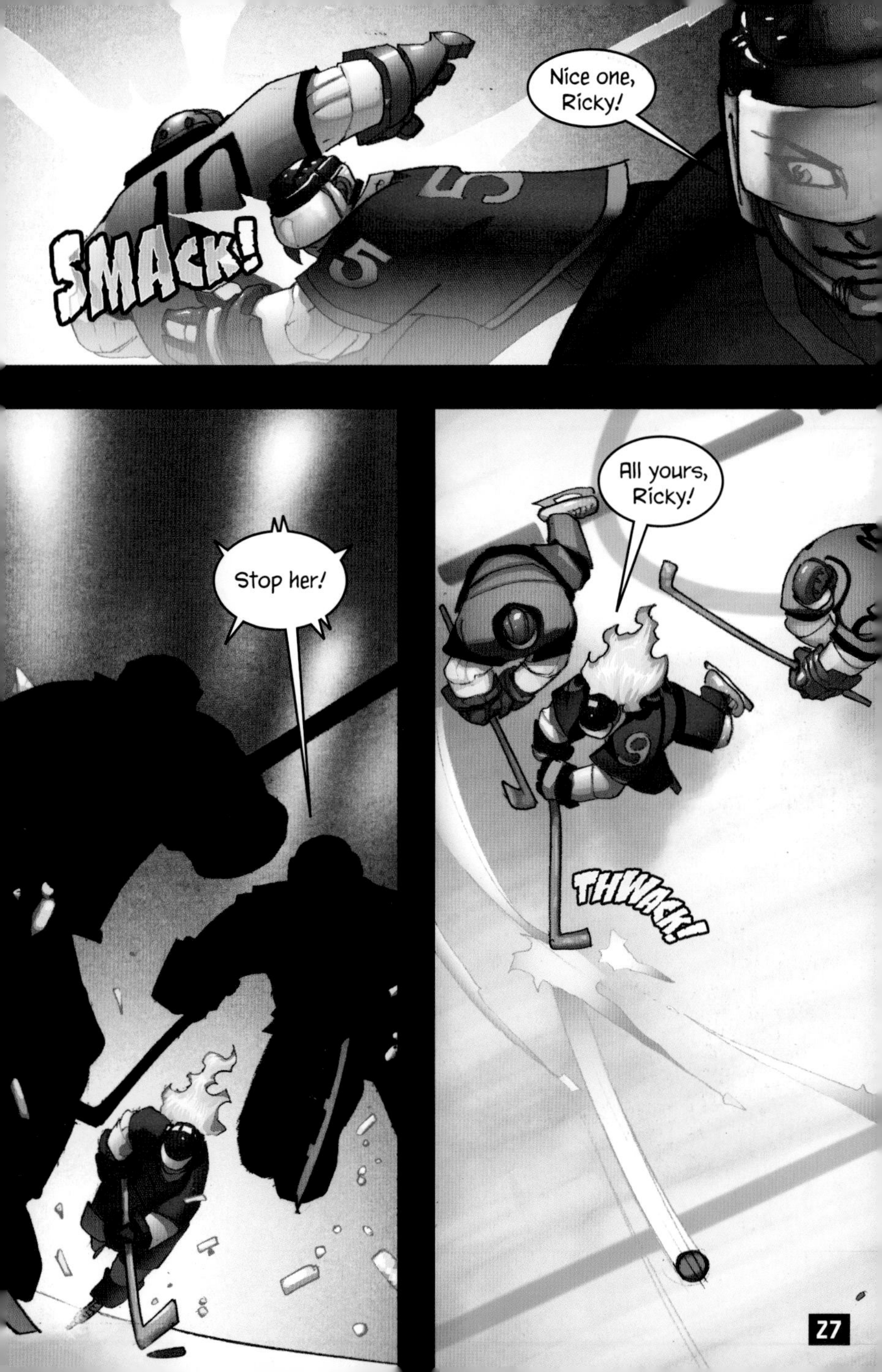
Nice one, Ricky!
SMACK!
Stop her!
All yours, Ricky!
THWACK!

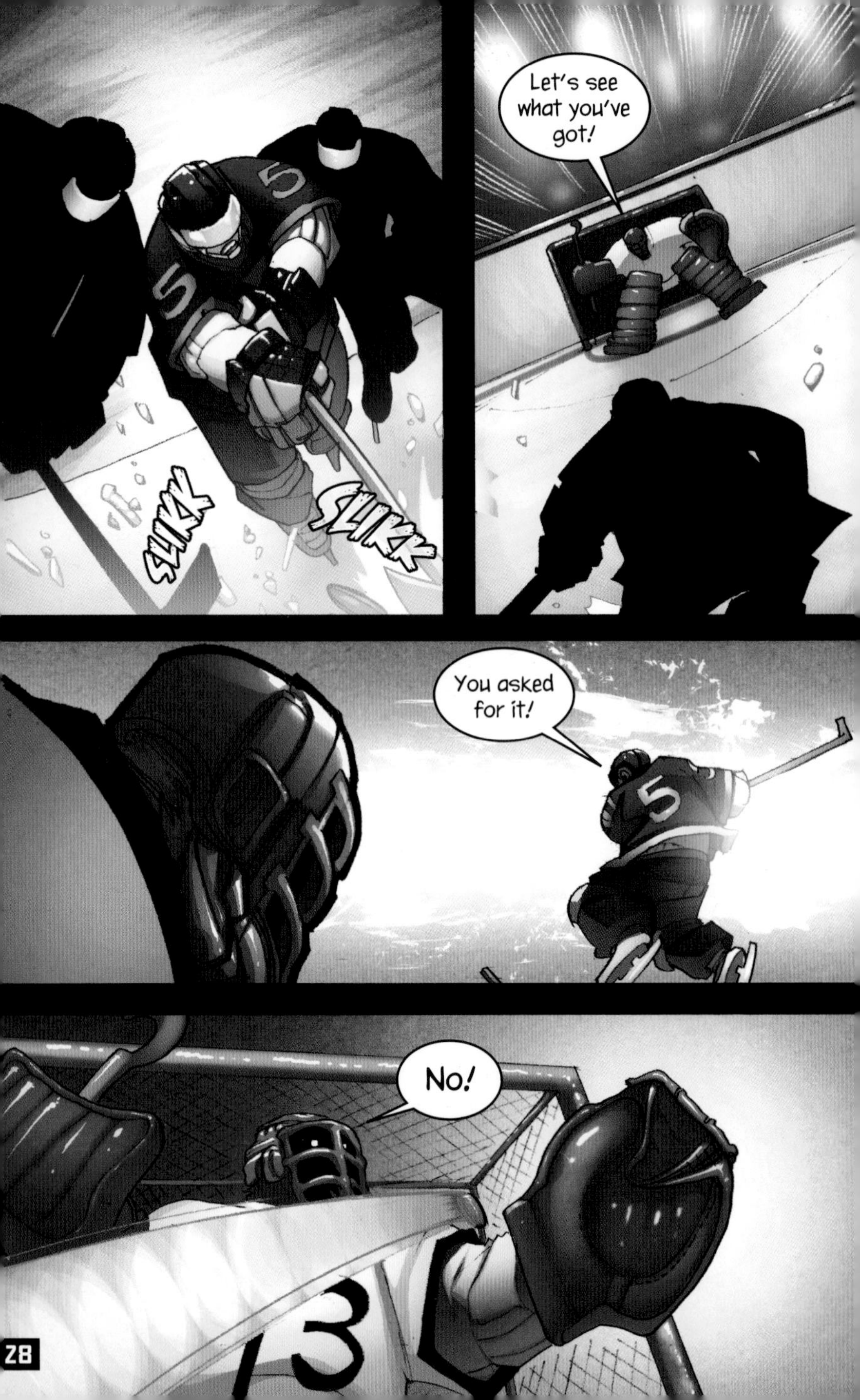

SLIKK
SLIKK
Let's see what you've got!
You asked for it!
No!

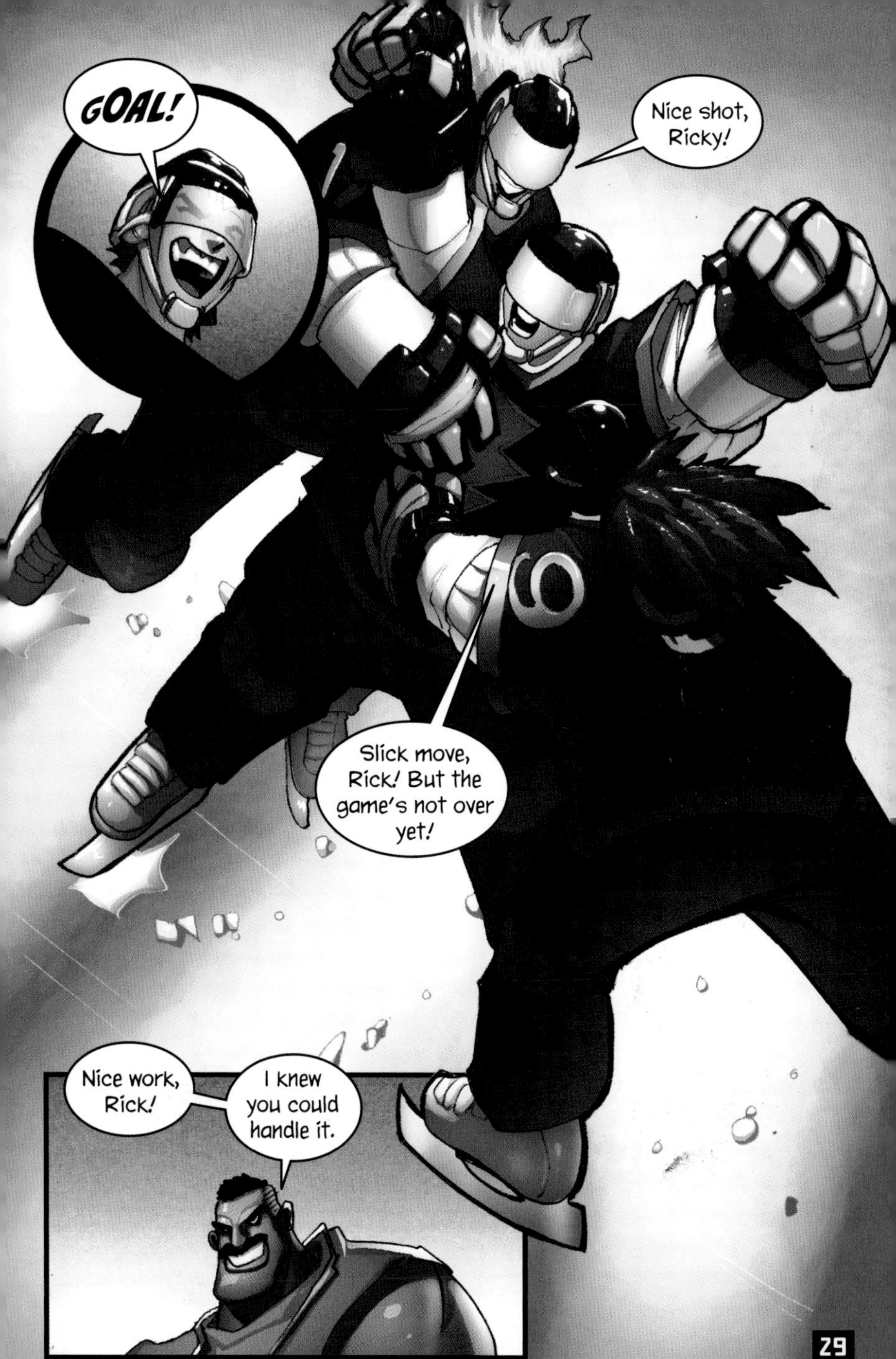
GOAL!
Nice shot, Ricky!
Slick move, Rick! But the game's not over yet!
Nice work, Rick!
I knew you could handle it.

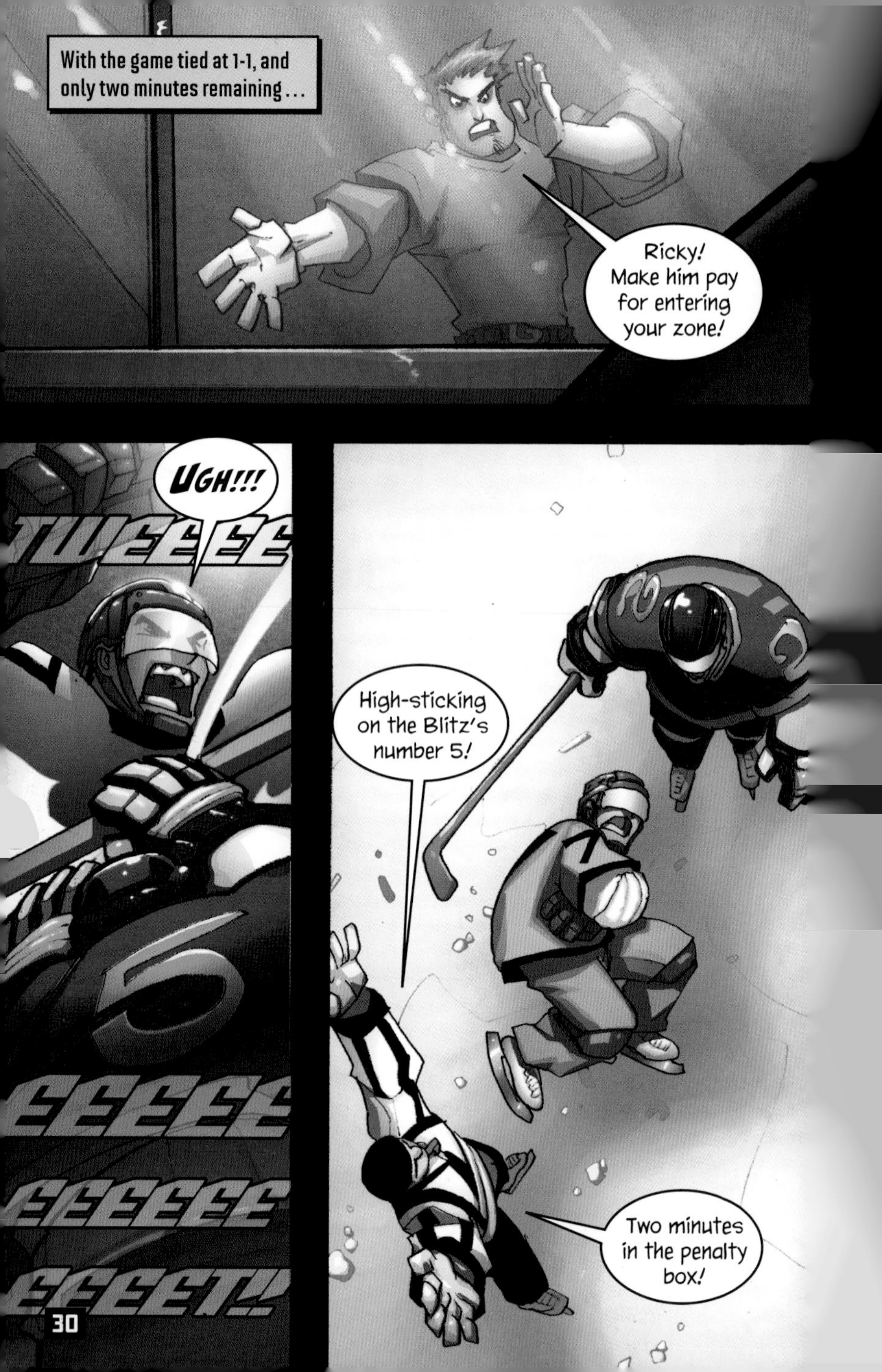
With the game tied at 1-1, and only two minutes remaining . . .
Ricky! Make him pay for entering your zone!
UGH!!!
TWEEEEEEEEEEEEEEEEEEET!!
High-sticking on the Blitz's number 5!
Two minutes in the penalty box!

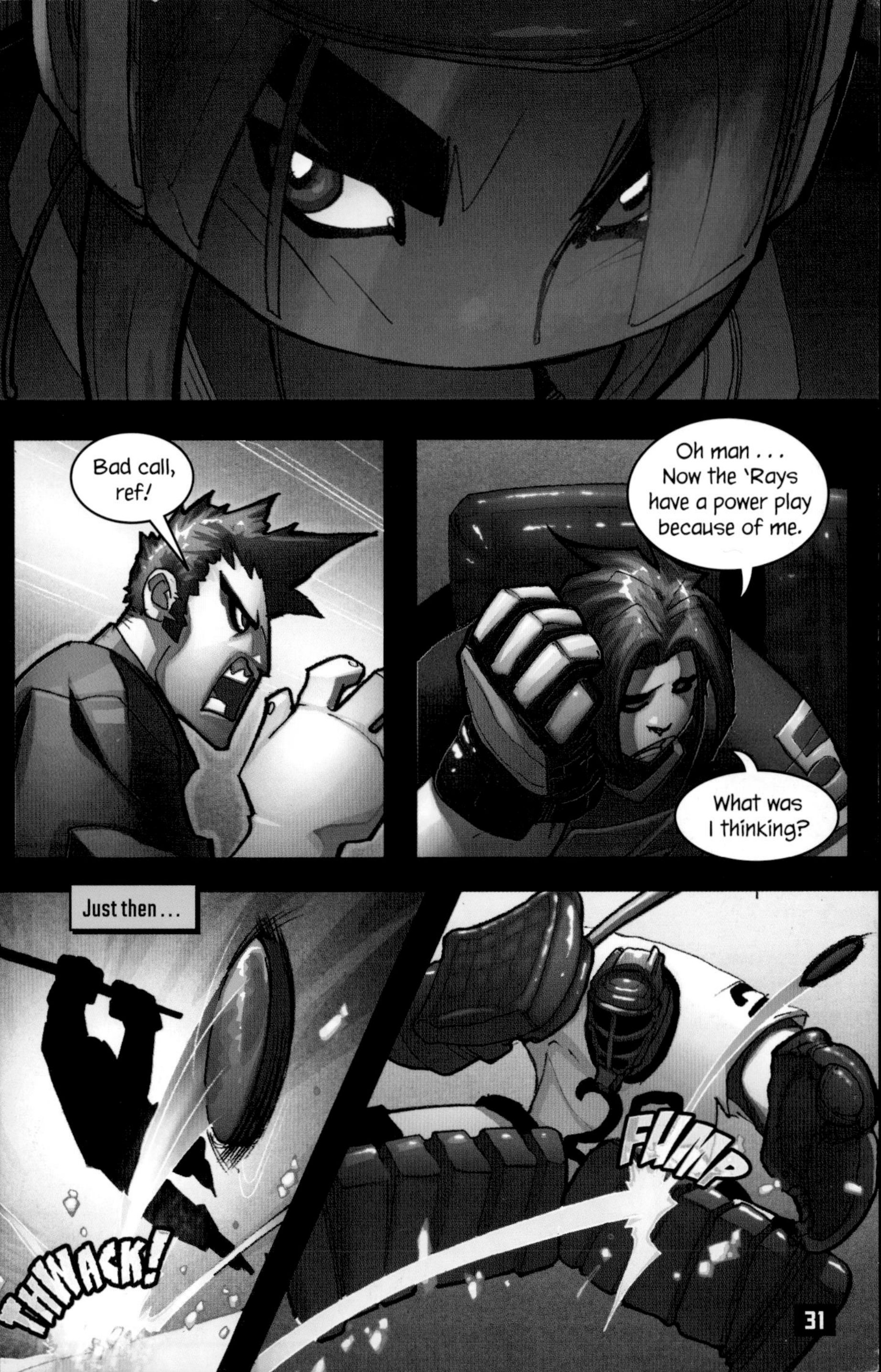

Bad call, ref!
Oh man . . . Now the 'Rays have a power play because of me.
What was I thinking?
Just then . . .
THWACK!
FUMP

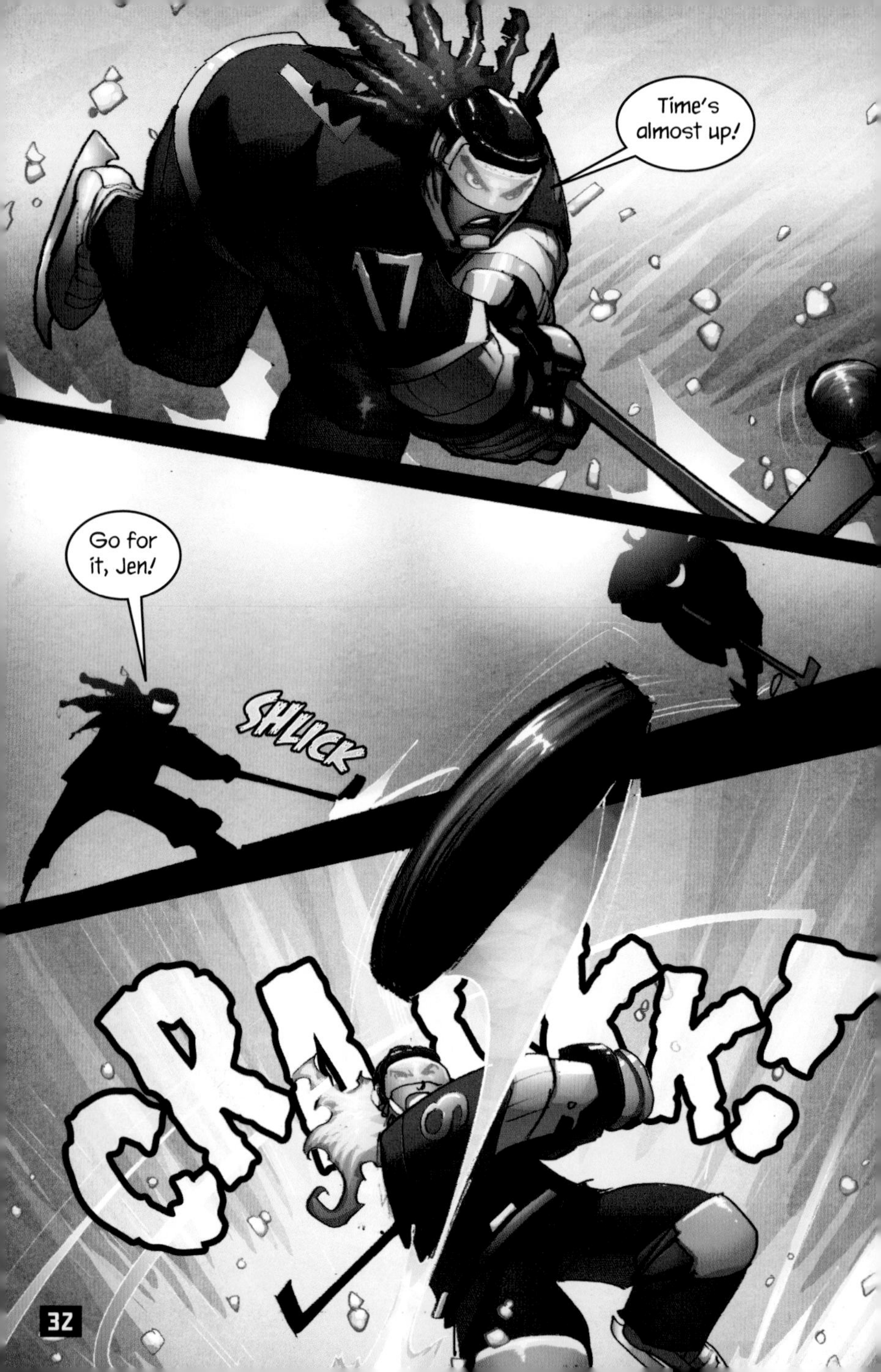
Time's almost up!
Go for it, Jen!
SHLICK

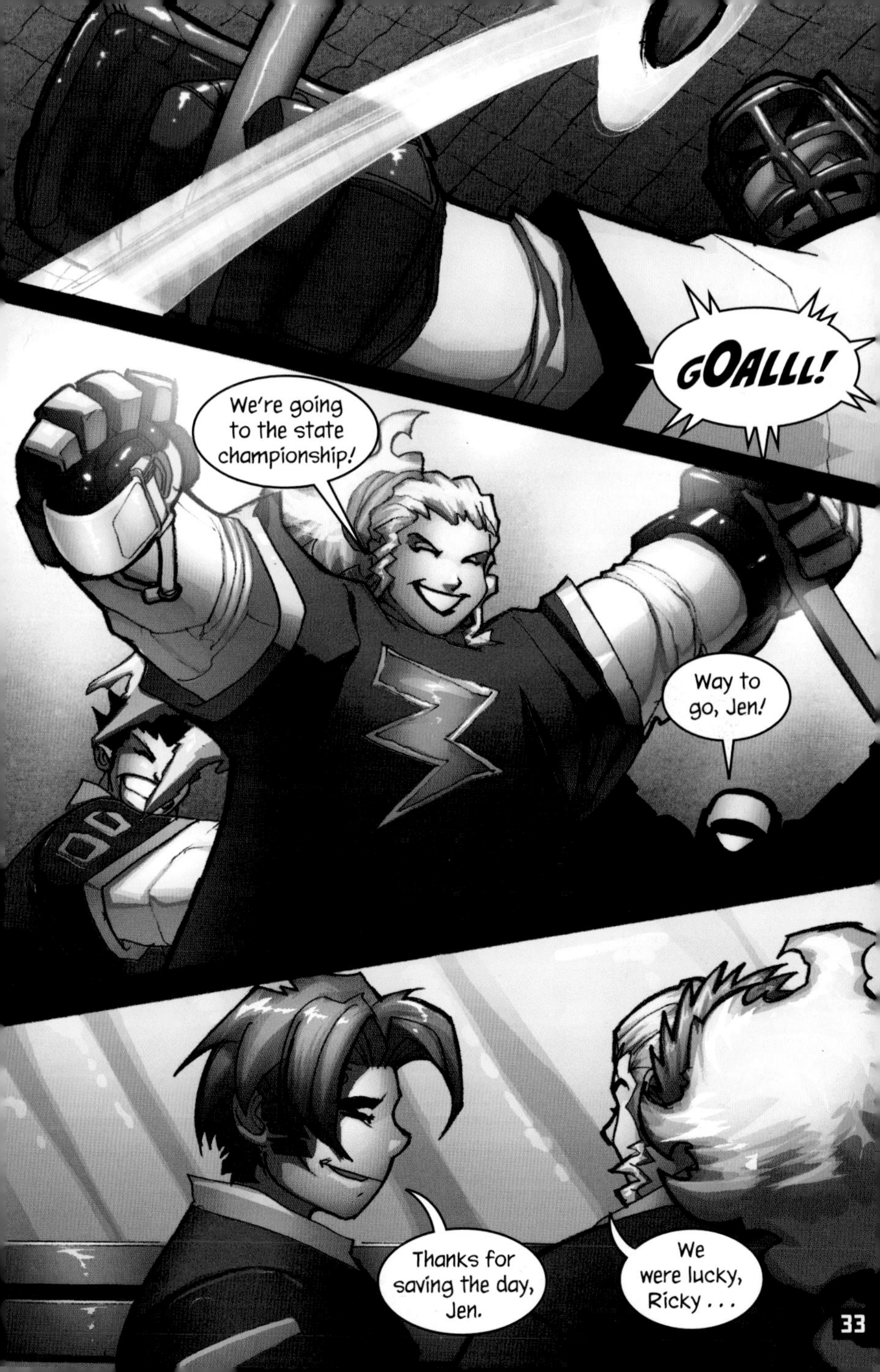
GOALLL!
We're going to the state championship!
Way to go, Jen!
Thanks for saving the day, Jen.
We were lucky, Ricky . . .

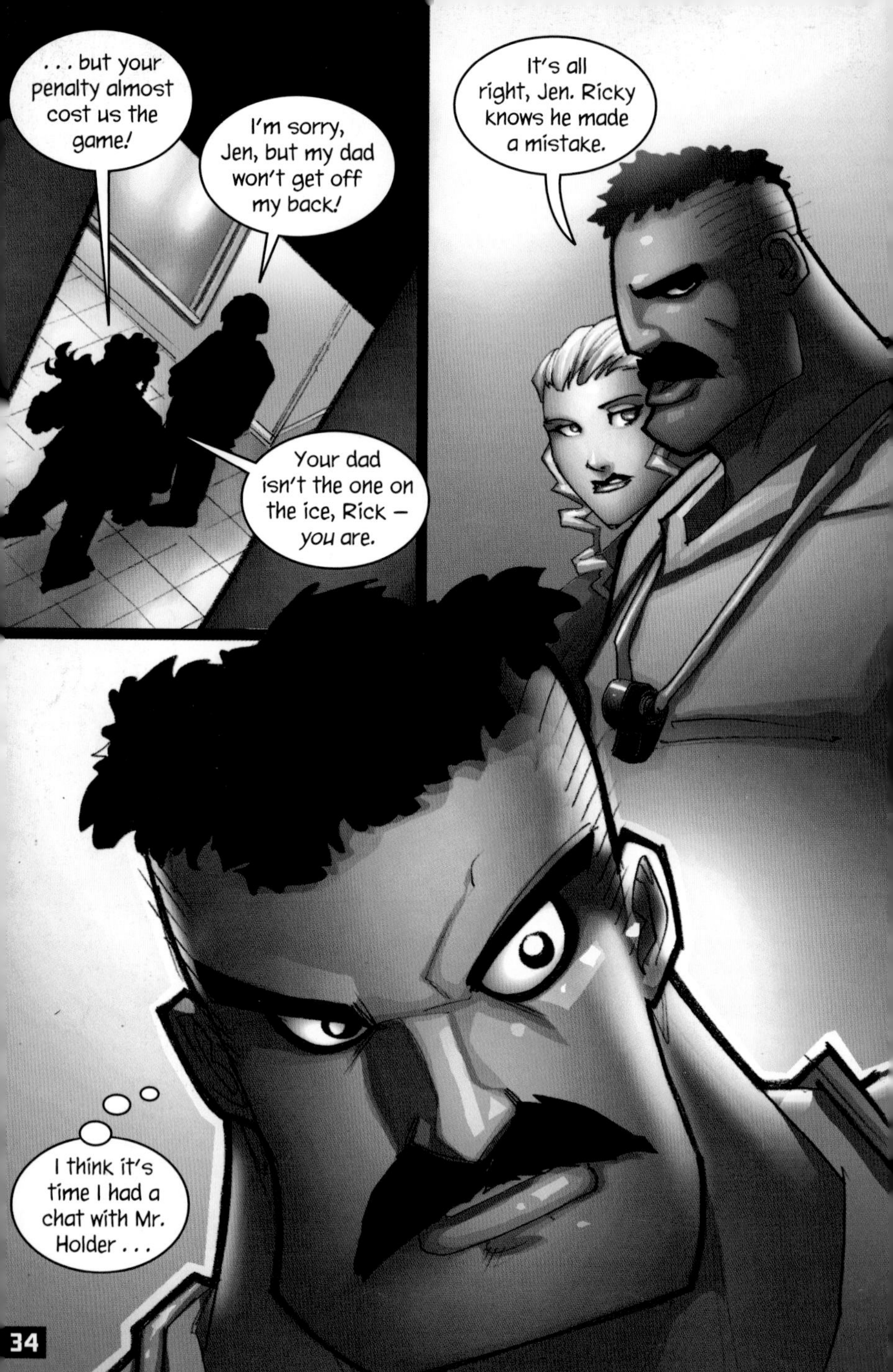
. . . but your penalty almost cost us the game!
I'm sorry, Jen, but my dad won't get off my back!
Your dad isn't the one on the ice, Rick — *you* are.
It's all right, Jen. Ricky knows he made a mistake.
I think it's time I had a chat with Mr. Holder . . .

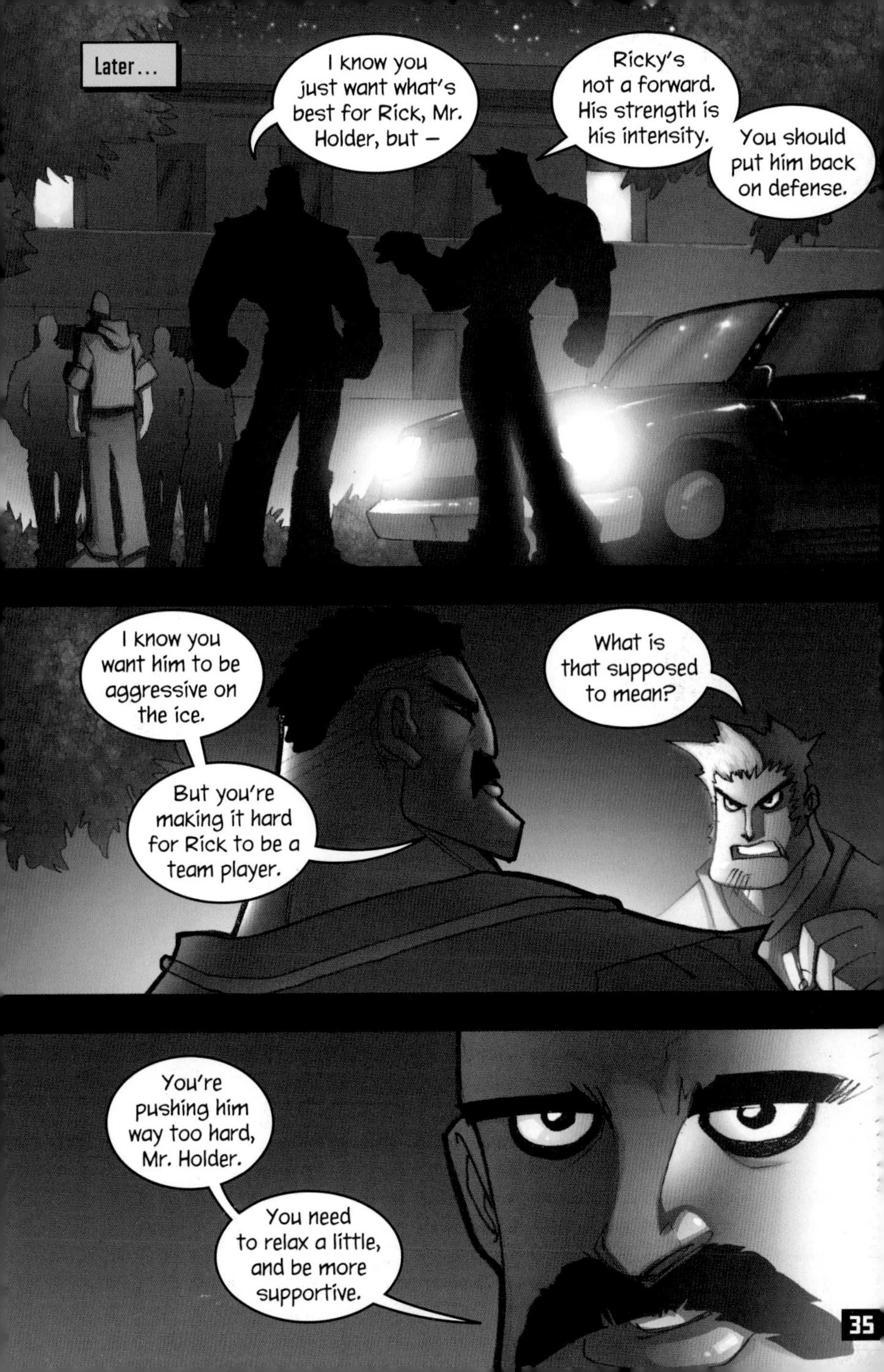
Later...
I know you just want what's best for Rick, Mr. Holder, but —
Ricky's not a forward. His strength is his intensity.
You should put him back on defense.
I know you want him to be aggressive on the ice.
But you're making it hard for Rick to be a team player.
What is that supposed to mean?
You're pushing him way too hard, Mr. Holder.
You need to relax a little, and be more supportive.

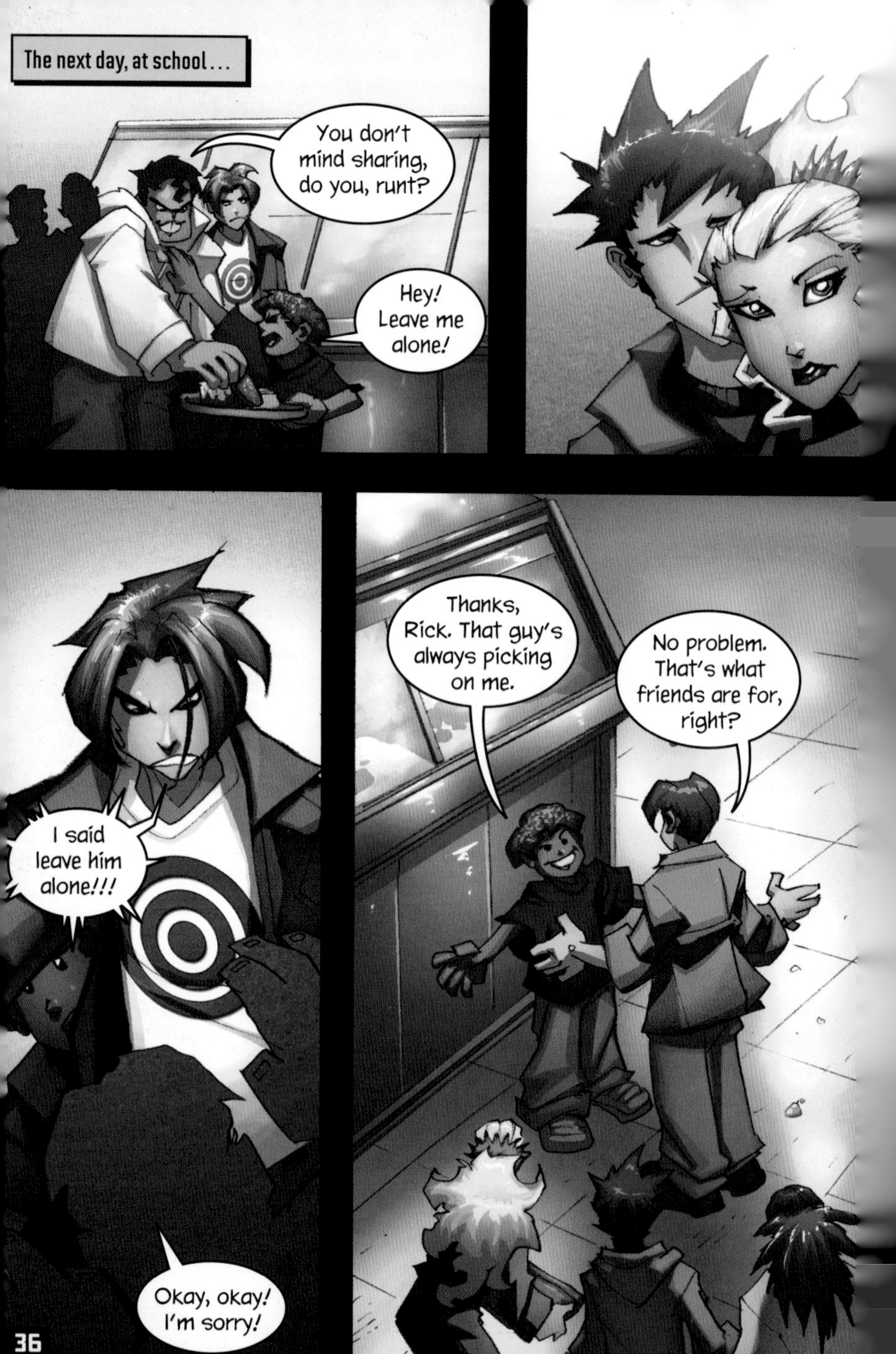
The next day, at school...
You don't mind sharing, do you, runt?
Hey! Leave me alone!
I said leave him alone!!!
Okay, okay! I'm sorry!
Thanks, Rick. That guy's always picking on me.
No problem. That's what friends are for, right?

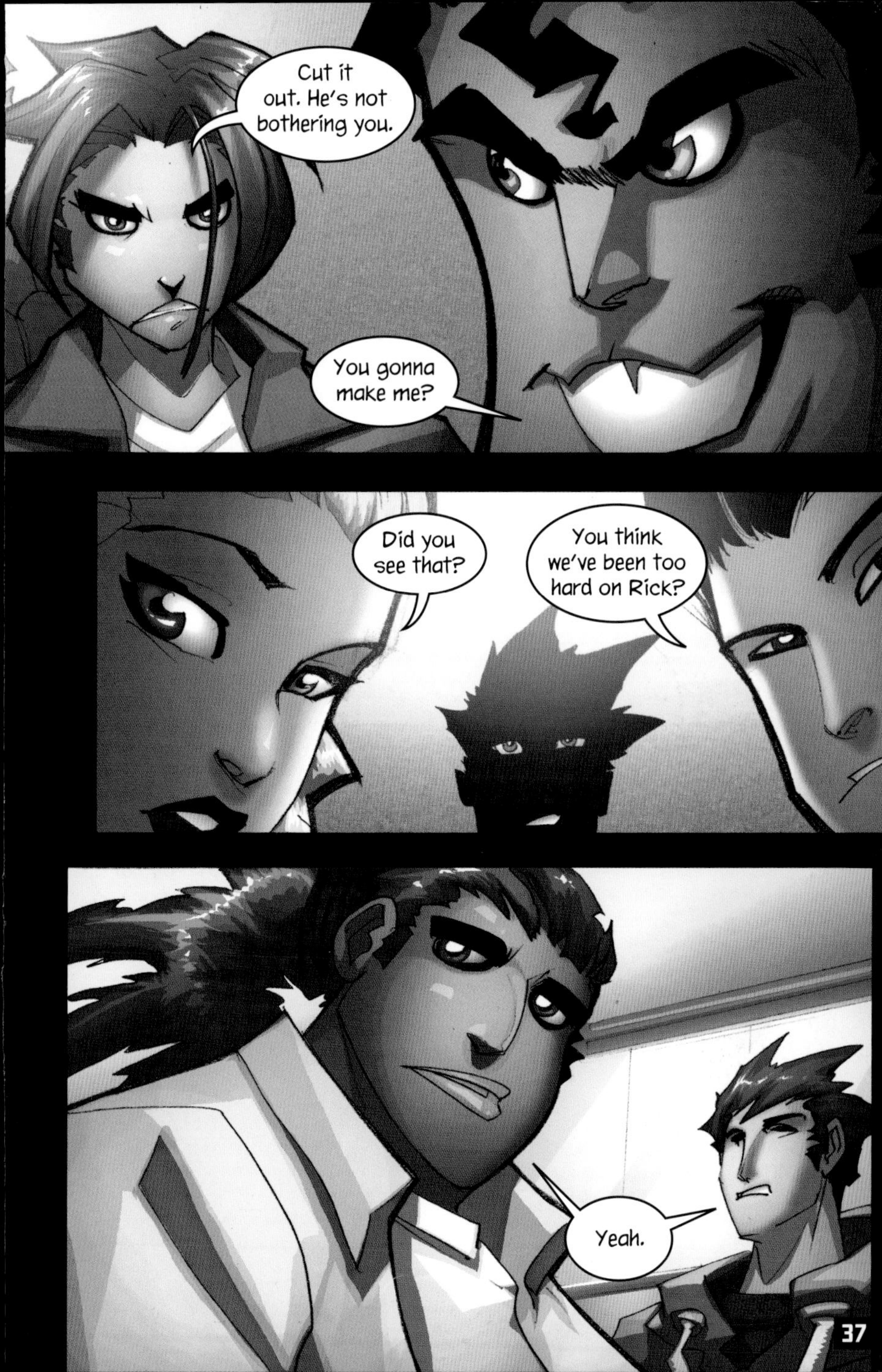
Cut it out. He's not bothering you.
You gonna make me?
Did you see that?
You think we've been too hard on Rick?
Yeah.

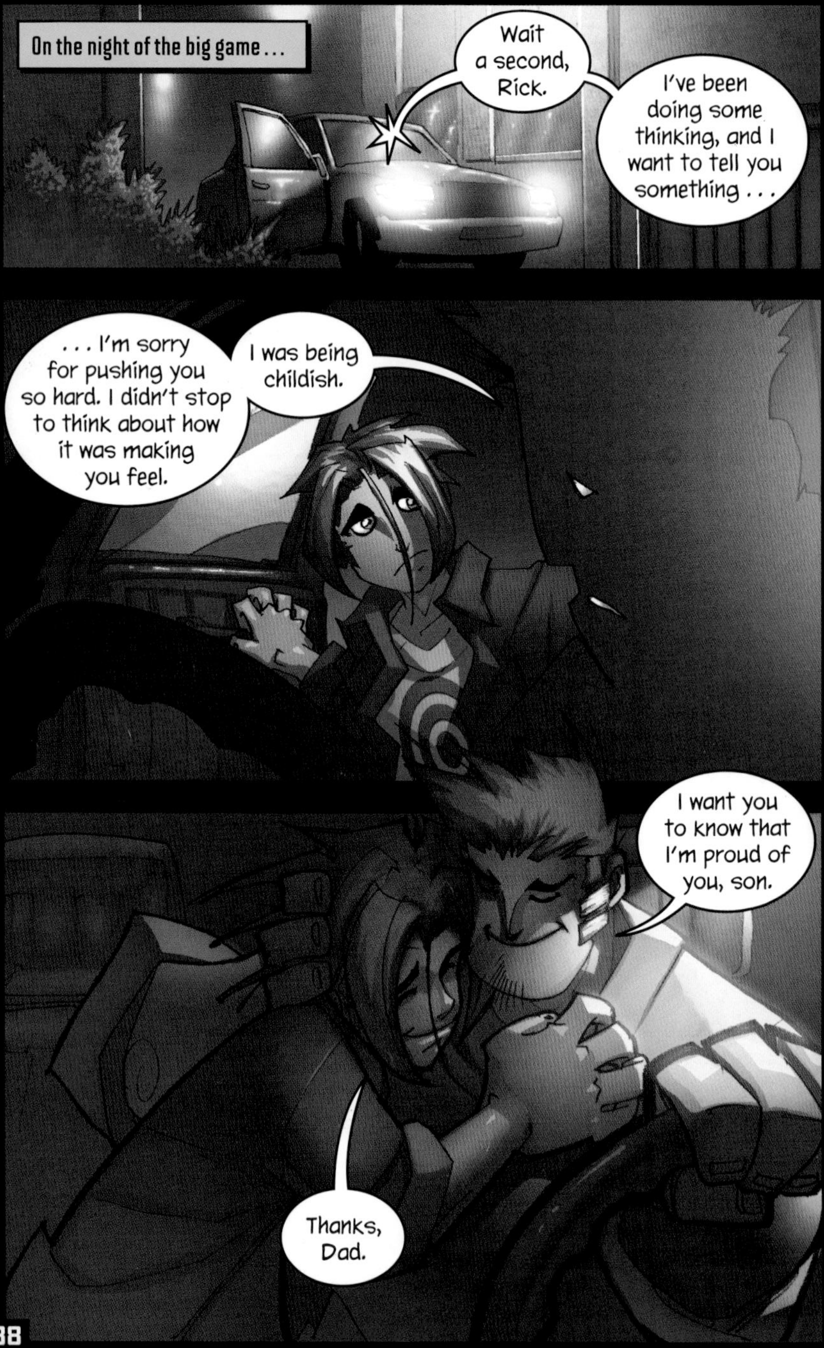
On the night of the big game . . .
Wait a second, Rick.
I've been doing some thinking, and I want to tell you something . . .
. . . I'm sorry for pushing you so hard. I didn't stop to think about how it was making you feel.
I was being childish.
I want you to know that I'm proud of you, son.
Thanks, Dad.

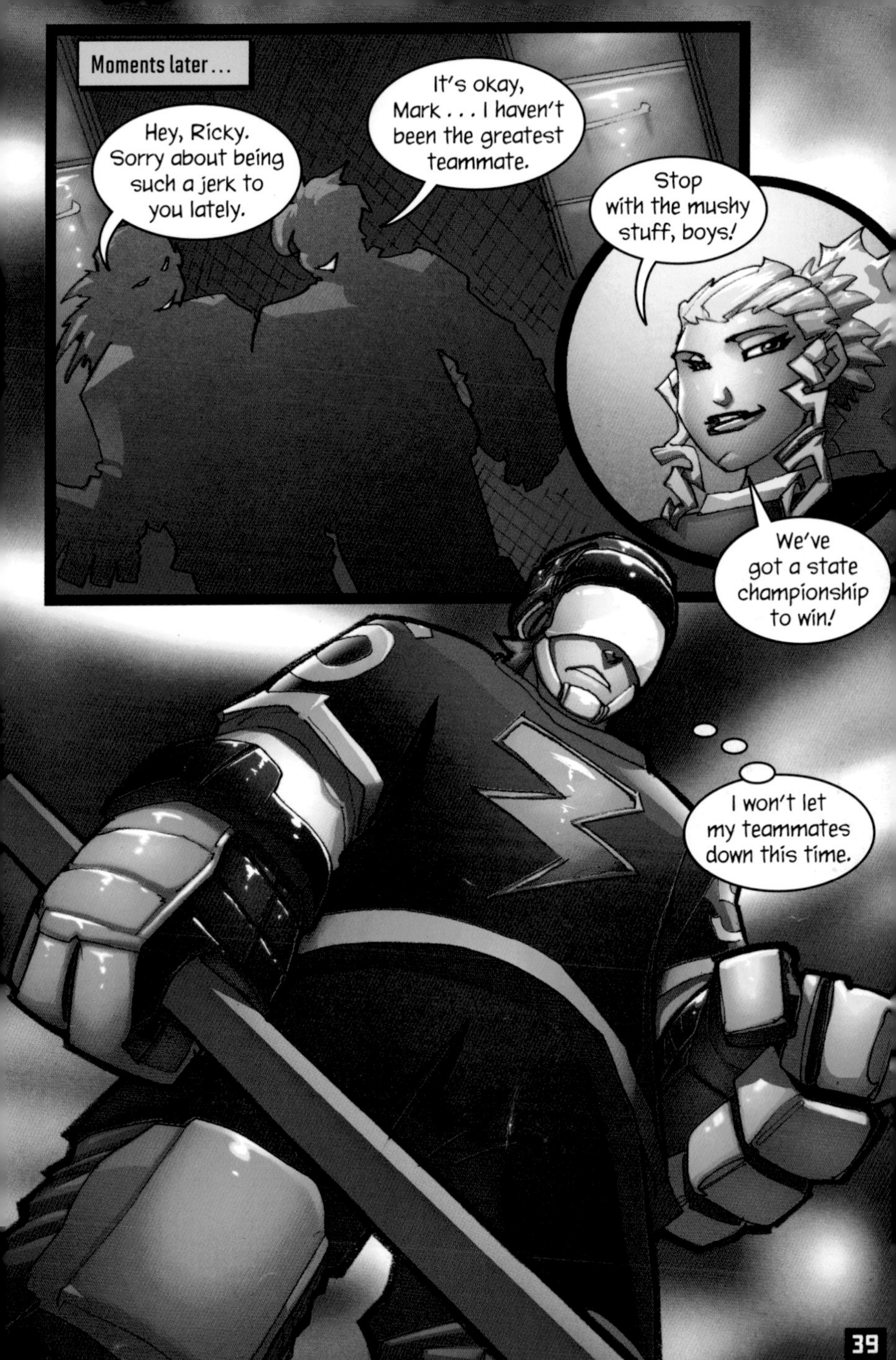
Moments later . . .
Hey, Ricky. Sorry about being such a jerk to you lately.
It's okay, Mark . . . I haven't been the greatest teammate.
Stop with the mushy stuff, boys!
We've got a state championship to win!
I won't let my teammates down this time.

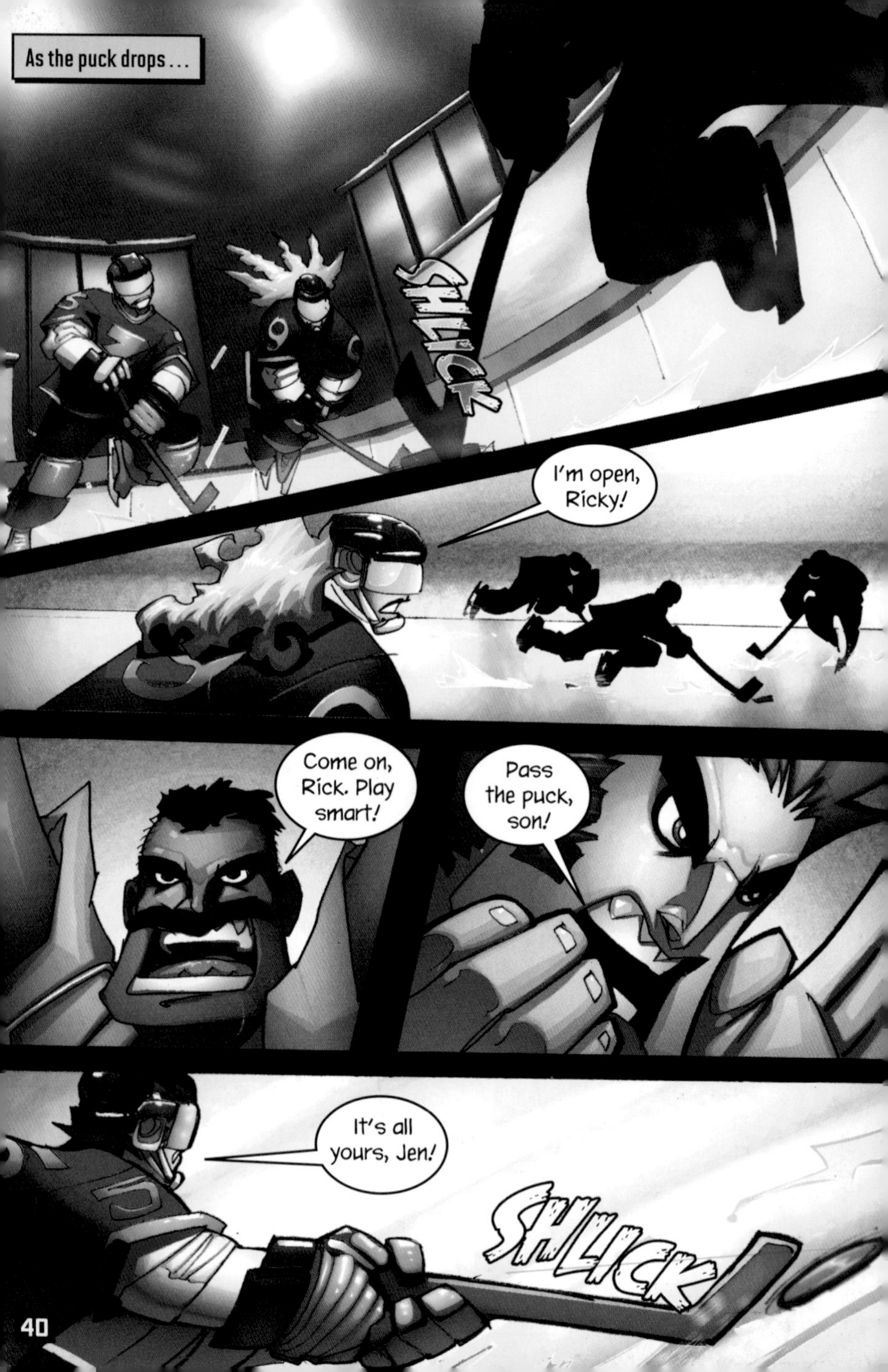
As the puck drops . . .
SHLICK
I'm open, Ricky!
Come on, Rick. Play smart!
Pass the puck, son!
It's all yours, Jen!
SHLICK

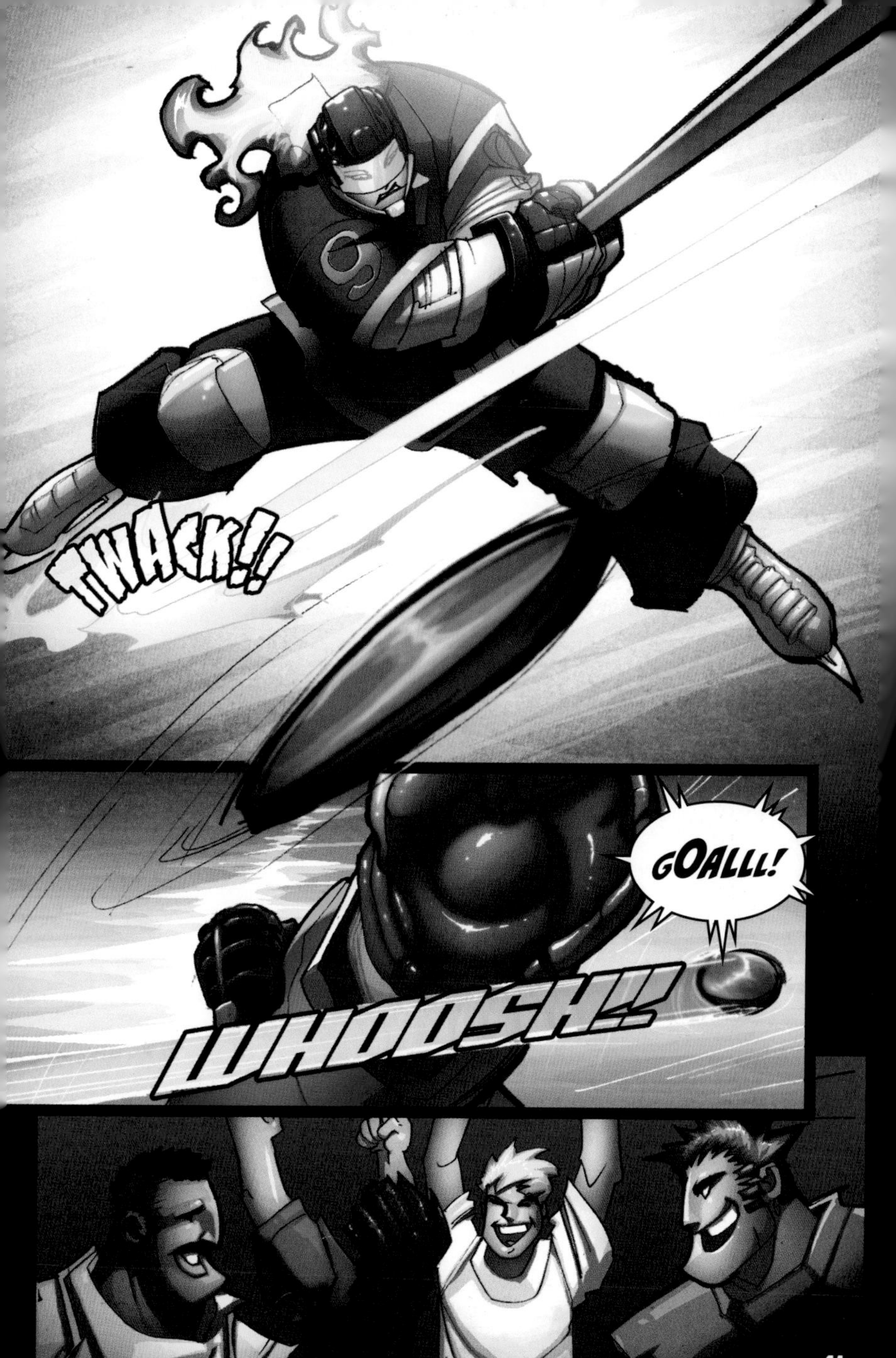
TWACK!!
GOALLL!
WHOOSH!!

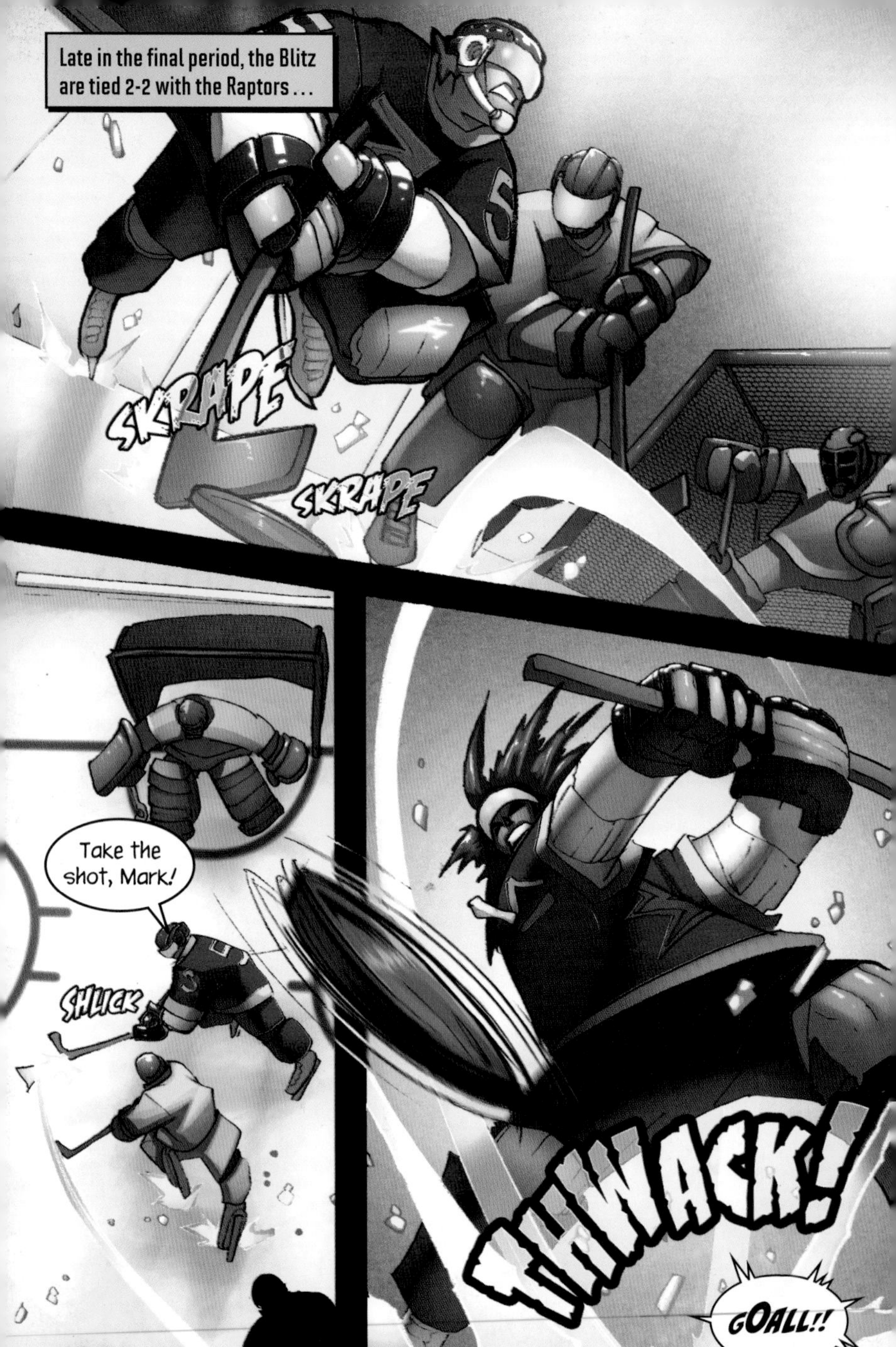
Late in the final period, the Blitz are tied 2-2 with the Raptors . . .
SKRAPE
SKRAPE
Take the shot, Mark!
SHLICK
THWACK!
GOALL!!

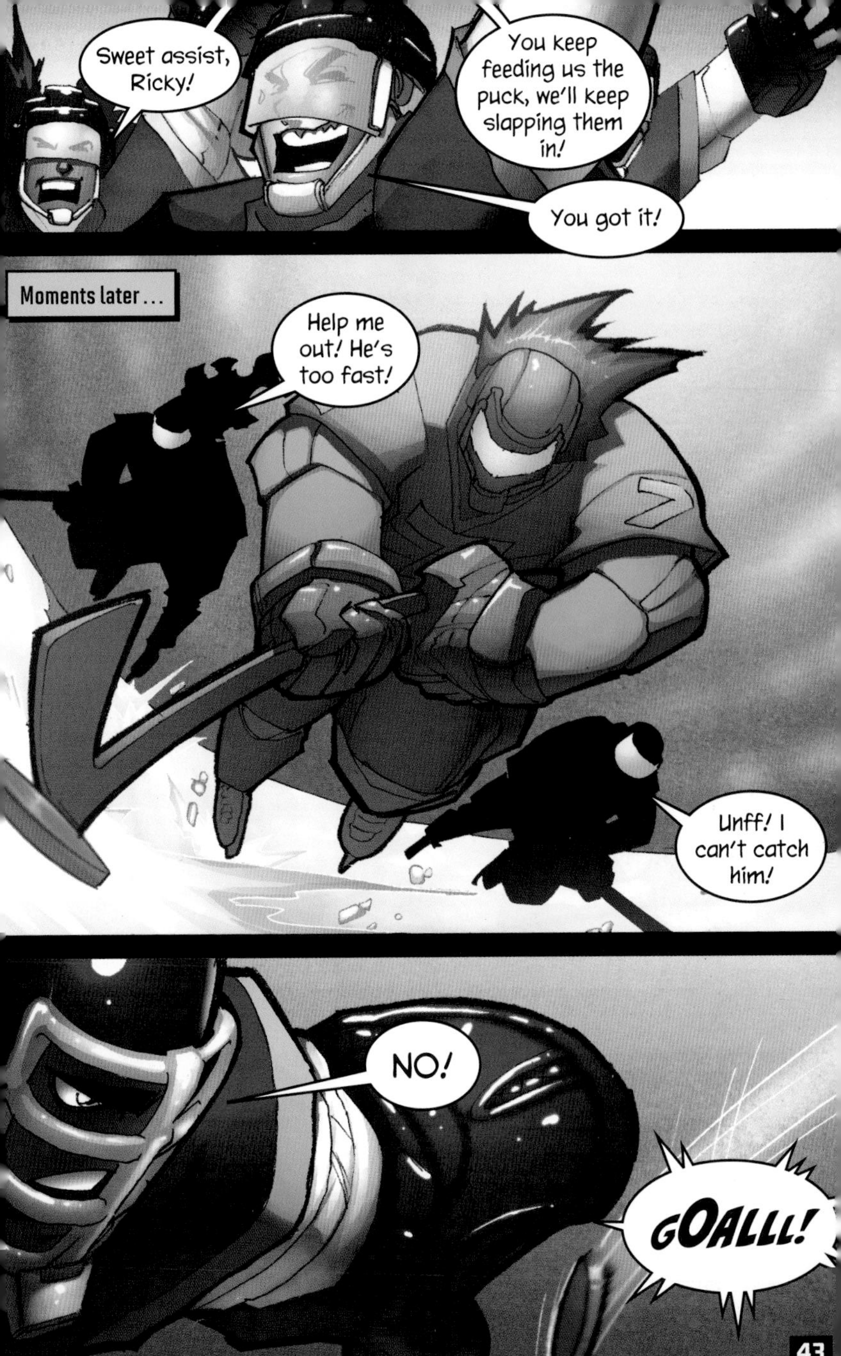
Sweet assist, Ricky!
You keep feeding us the puck, we'll keep slapping them in!
You got it!
Moments later . . .
Help me out! He's too fast!
Unff! I can't catch him!
NO!
GOALLL!

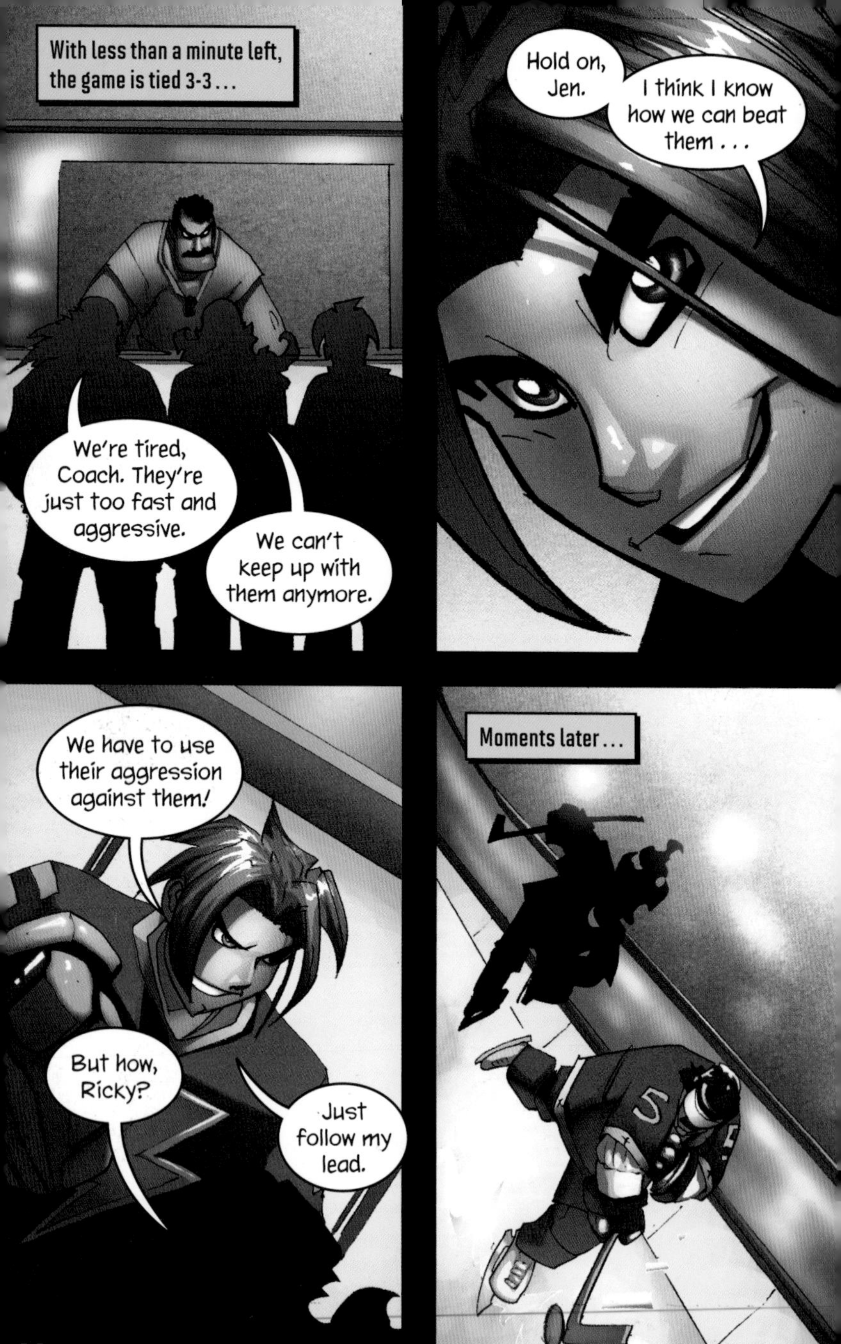
With less than a minute left, the game is tied 3-3 . . .
We're tired, Coach. They're just too fast and aggressive.
We can't keep up with them anymore.
Hold on, Jen.
I think I know how we can beat them . . .
We have to use their aggression against them!
But how, Ricky?
Just follow my lead.
Moments later . . .

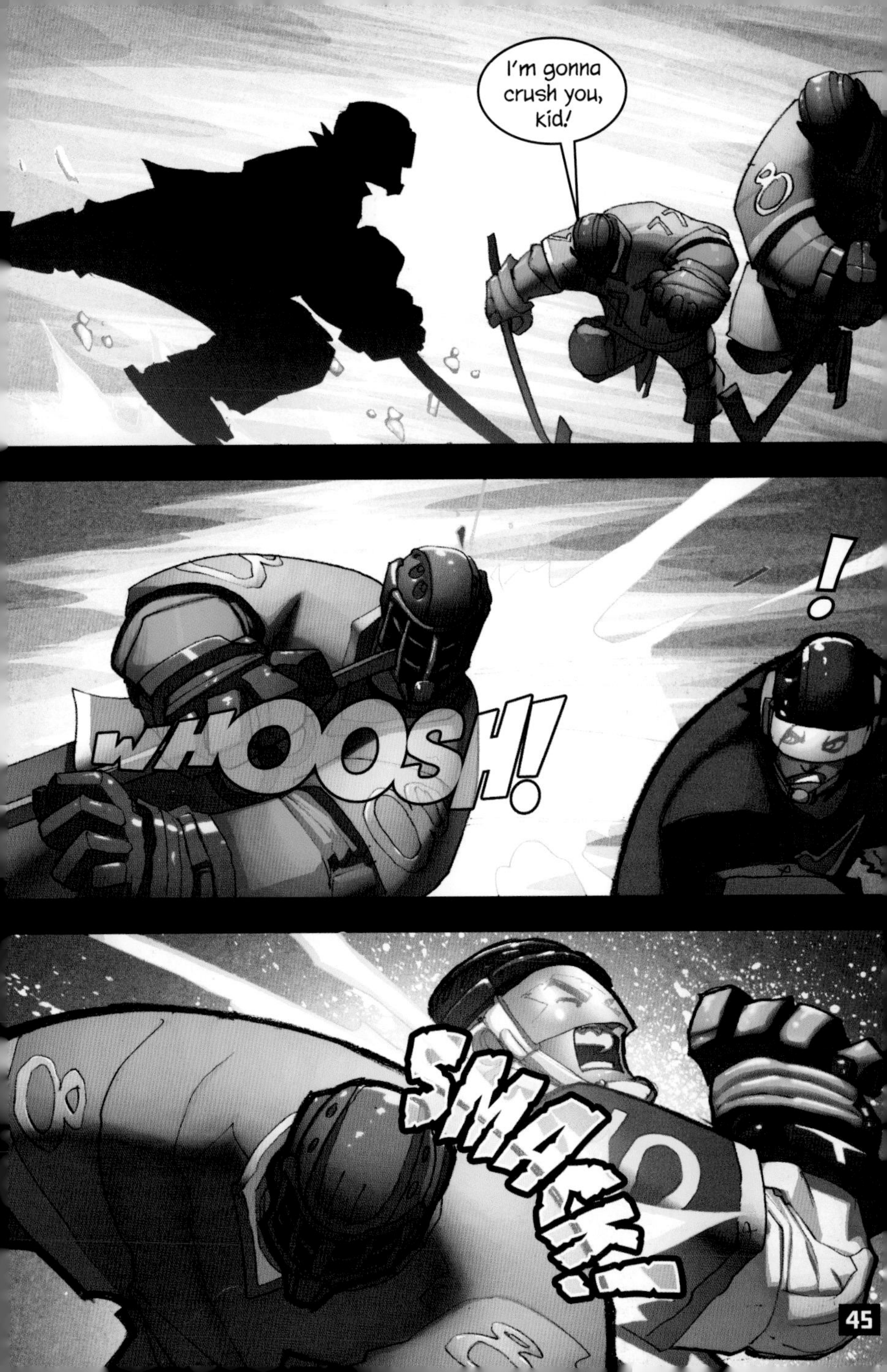
I'm gonna crush you, kid!
WHOOSH!
!
SMACK!

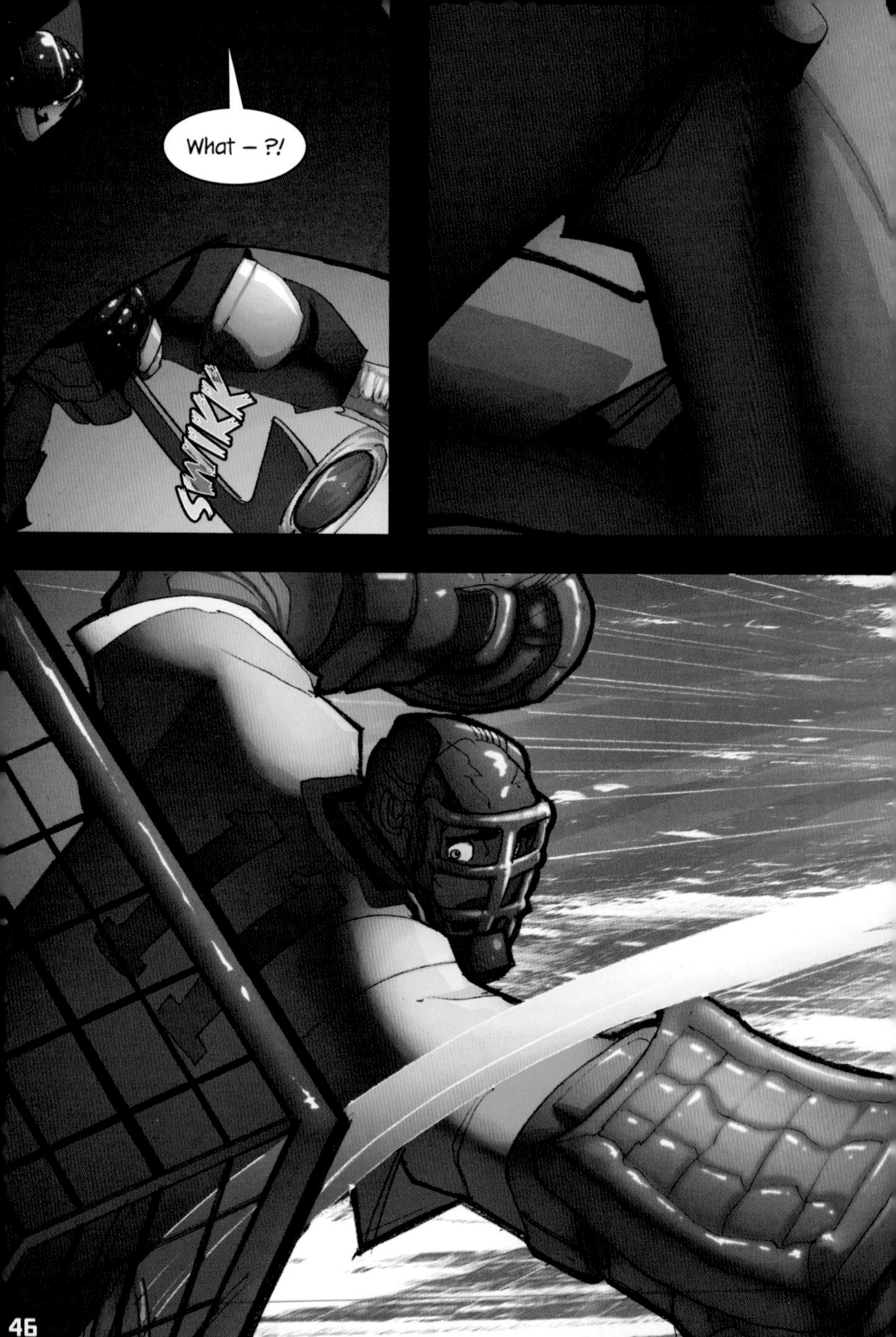
What — ?!
SWIKK

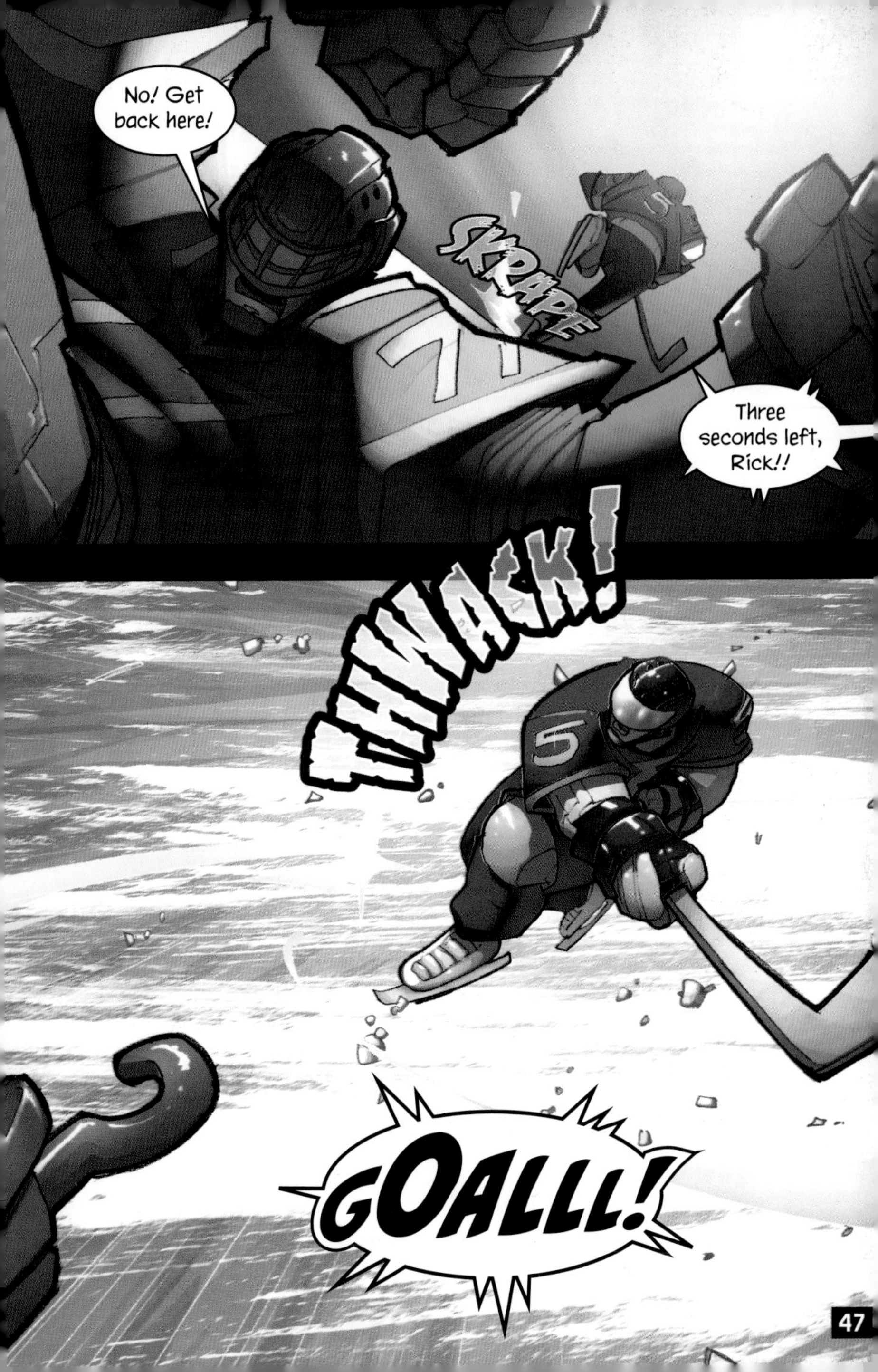
No! Get back here!
SKRAPE
Three seconds left, Rick!!
THWACK!
GOALLL!

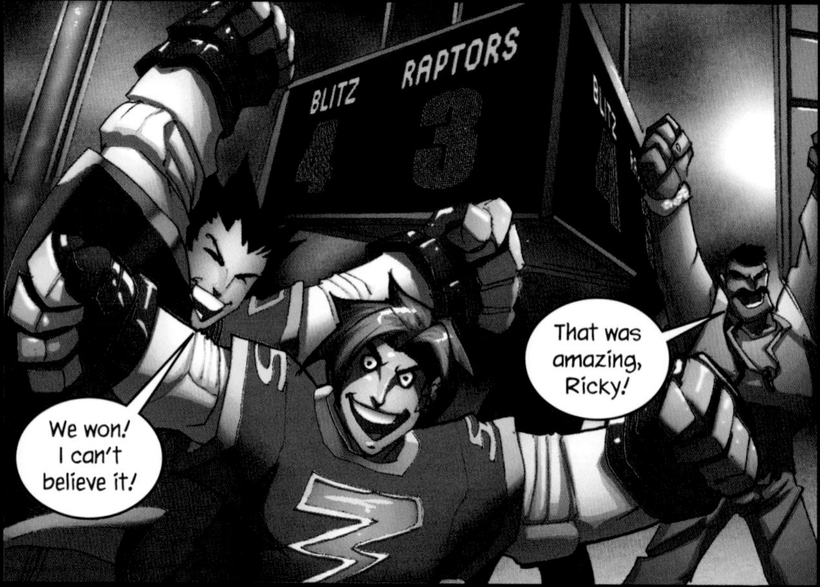
BLITZ
RAPTORS
3
We won! I can't believe it!
That was amazing, Ricky!

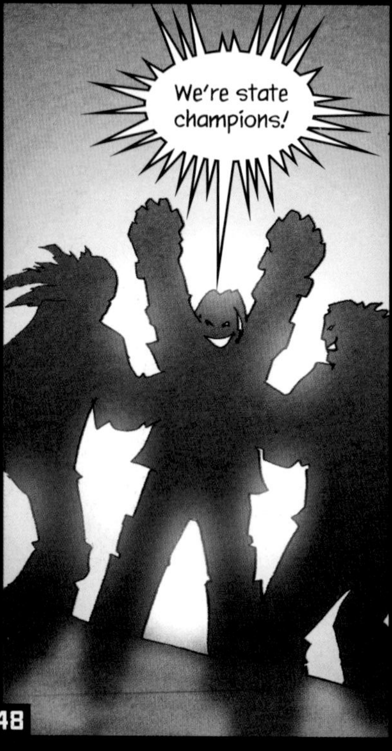
We're state champions!

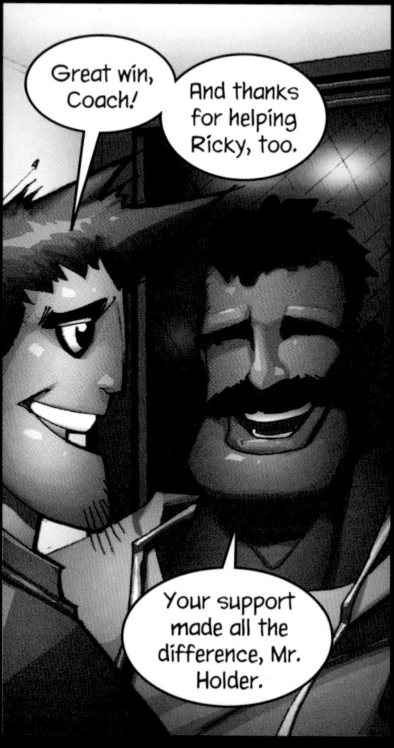
Great win, Coach!
And thanks for helping Ricky, too.
Your support made all the difference, Mr. Holder.

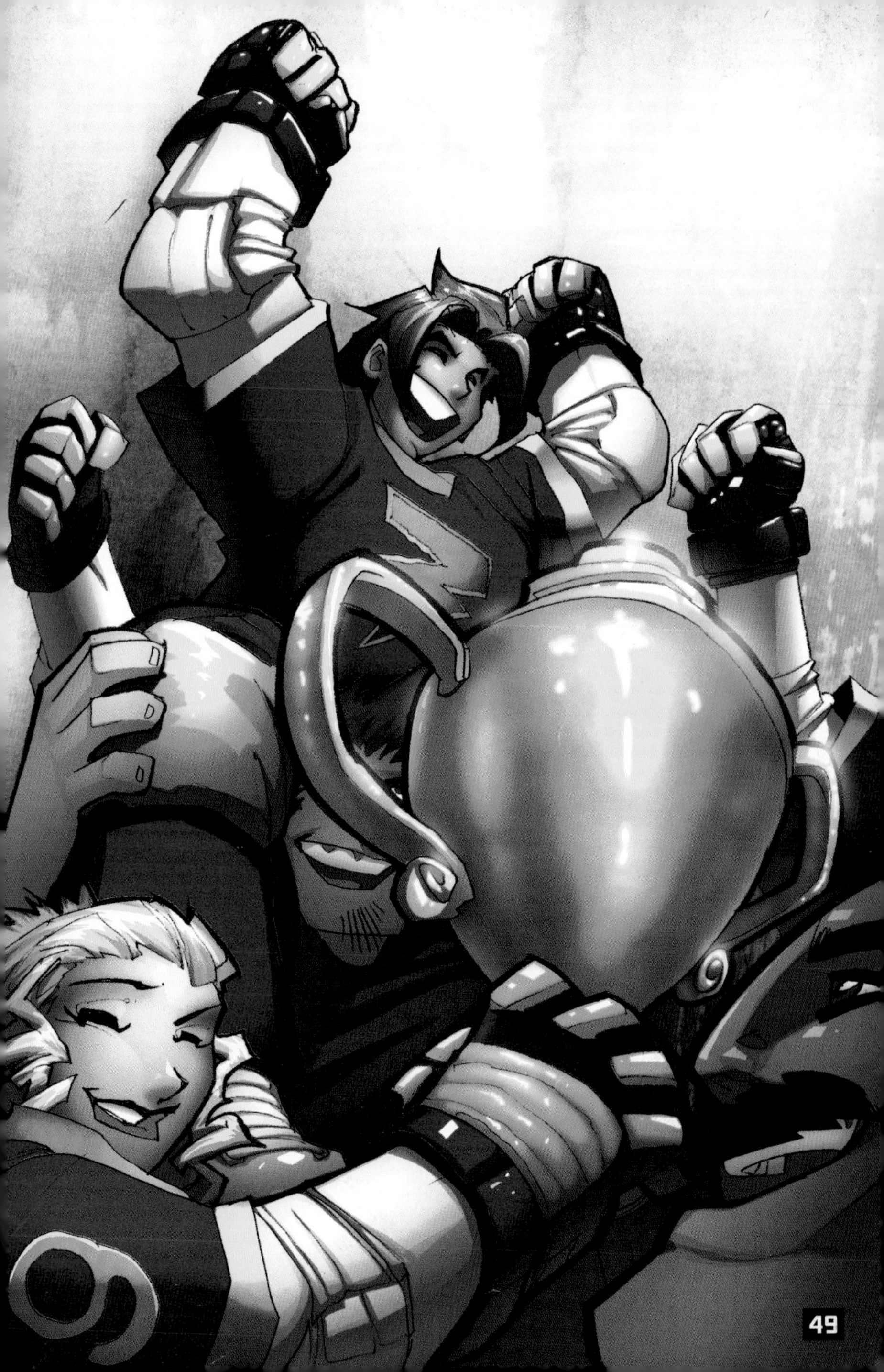

SPORTS ZONE
POSTGAME RECAP

HKY
HOCKEY

PNT
PAINTBALL

SKT
SKATEBOARDING

BSL
BASEBALL

BBL
BASKETBALL

HOLDER

BLITZ

RICKY'S REALITY CHECK EARNS HIM TEAM MVP — AND *THE STATE TITLE!*

BY THE NUMBERS

FINAL SCORE:
BLITZ 4, RAPTORS 3

SEASON HIGHS:
GOALS: TAYLOR, 22
ASSISTS: HOLDER, 31
HAT TRICKS: JACOBS, 2

STORY:
In a shocking move, Coach Morelli moved the overly aggressive Holder from defenseman to right wing minutes before the big game. The risky switch paid off — Ricky was able to put his anger on ice, and went on to score the championship-winning goal. After the game, Ricky was named team MVP in a unanimous vote by his Blitz teammates.

Sports Illustrated KIDS

UP NEXT: SI KIDS INFO CENTER

SZ POSTGAME EXT

WHERE *YOU* ANALYZE THE GAME!

Hockey fans were treated to an amazing game today when Ricky H the Blitz ran right over the Raptors. Let's go into the stands and fans for their perspectives on today's exciting championship game

DISCUSSION QUESTION 1

Ricky gets different advice from his friends and from his father. Who gives you better advice — your parents, or your friends? Why?

DISCUSSION QUESTION 2

Mr. Holder puts a lot of pressure on his son, Ricky. How do you handle pressure? Can pressure ever be a good thing? Why or why not?

WRITING PROMPT 1

Ricky feels trapped between his father's and his friends' expectations. Have you ever felt trapped? What was the situation? What did you do about it?

WRITING PROMPT 2

Did Ricky's teammates handle his aggressive behavior the right way? What could they have done better? How can you help an angry friend?

POWERED B
OLDER GOES FROM SKATING ON THIN ICE TO HOLDING A TROPHY MID-RINK

Sports Illustrated KIDS

INFO CENTER

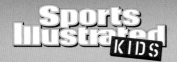

GLOSSARY

AGGRESSIVE (uh-GRESS-iv)—making a forceful, total effort to win or succeed

ASSIST (uh-SISST)—the pass made to a scoring player just before a goal. A maximum of two assists can be given per goal.

CHECK (CHEK)—a hit made by a defending player against an opponent in an attempt to get the puck away from them or slow them down

HIGH-STICKING (HI-STIK-ing)—penalty called when a player's stick is raised above the waist when they contact another player

INTENSITY (in-TEN-suh-tee)—showing great energy, strength, or focus in a competition of some sort

RESPONSIBLE (ri-SPON-suh-buhl)—if you are responsible for something, then you caused it to happen

SCRIMMAGE (SKRIM-ij)—a game played for practice, usually with one team dividing its players into two opposing teams

VOLUNTEERED (vol-uhn-TEERD)—offered to do something, usually for no reward

EATORS

NEL YOMTOV › *Author*

The career path of Nel Yomtov has taken him from the halls of Marvel Comics, as an editor, writer, and colorist, to the world of toy development. He then became editorial and art director at a children's nonfiction book publisher. Now, Nel is a writer and editor of books, websites, and graphic novels for children. A harmonica-honking blues enthusiast, Nel lives in New York with his wife, Nancy. They have a son, Jess.

GERARDO SANDOVAL › *Illustrator*

Gerardo Sandoval is a professional comic book illustrator from Mexico. He has worked on many well-known comics, including Tomb Raider books from Top Cow Production. He has also worked on designs for posters and card sets.

BENNY FUENTES › *Colorist*

Benny Fuentes lives in Villahermosa, Tabasco in Mexico, where the temperature is just as hot as the sauce is. He works as a full-time colorist in the comic book industry for companies like Marvel, DC Comics, and Top Cow Productions. He shares his home with two crazy cats, Chelo and Kitty, who act like they own the place.

Sports Illustrated KIDS GRAPHIC NOVELS

QUICK COMIC

TOU YANG AND DARREN BRODY IN:

KICKOFF BLITZ

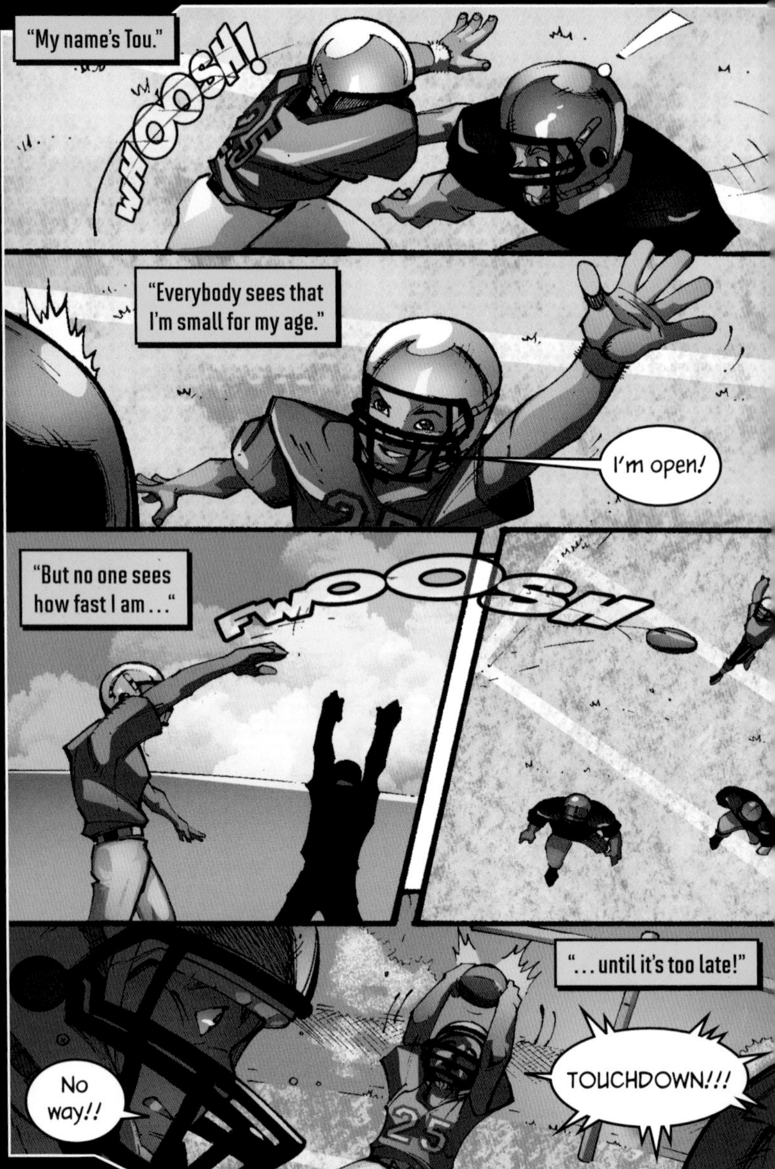
"My name's Tou."
WHOOSH!
"Everybody sees that I'm small for my age."
I'm open!
"But no one sees how fast I am . . ."
FWOOOSH
". . . until it's too late!"
No way!!
TOUCHDOWN!!!

» LOVE THIS QUICK COMIC? READ THE WHOLE STORY IN KICKOFF BLITZ – ONLY FROM STONE ARCH BOOKS!

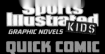

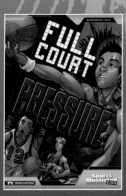

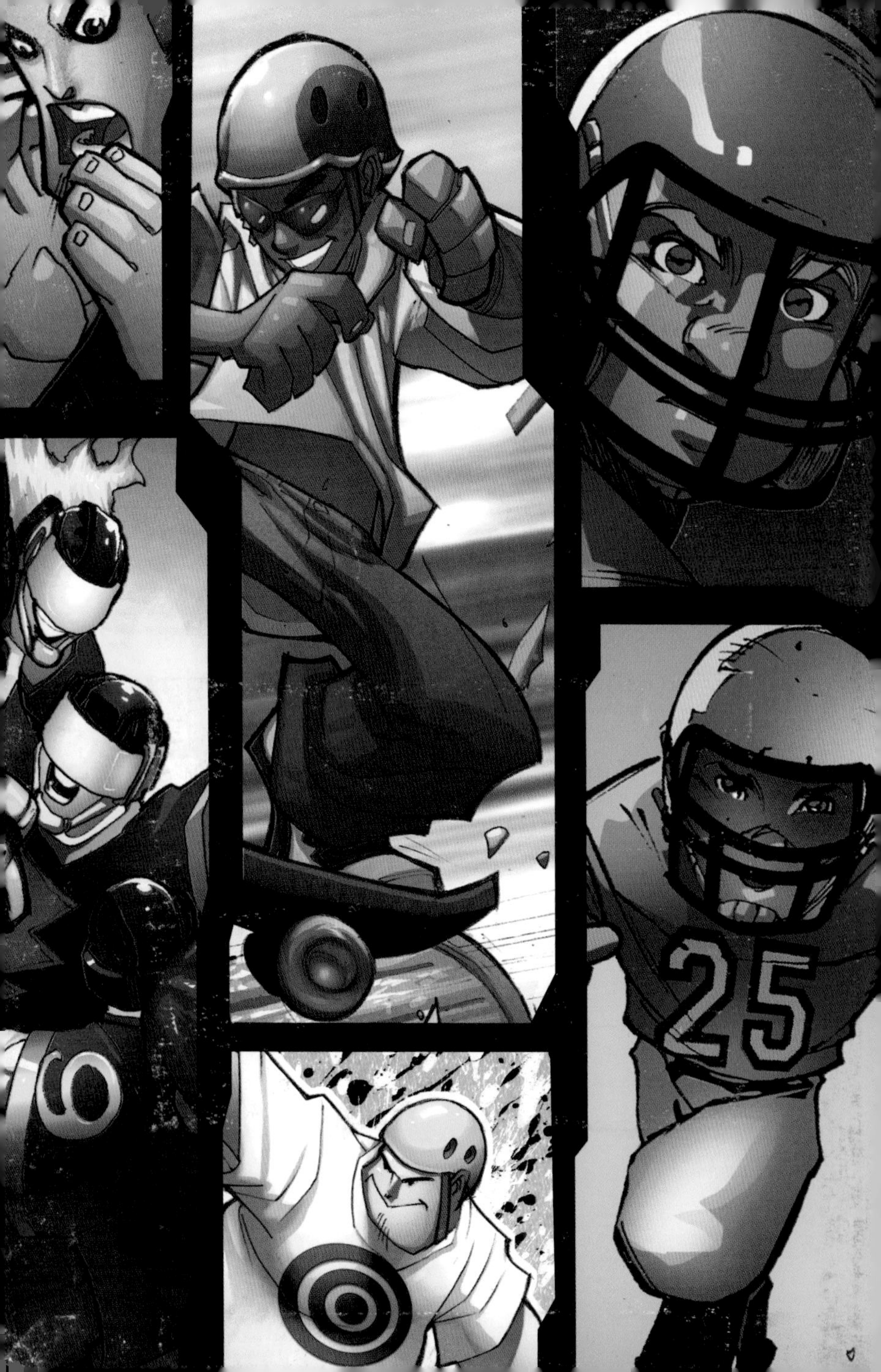
25